SHAYNE HIT THE DOOR AGAIN...

...this time lower and closer to the lock, and there was the protesting screech of screws being torn from wood and the door burst open, almost catapulting the detective forward on his face.

He caught the door-jamb and straightened himself slowly.

A thin, intense-faced young man with a lock of black hair slanted across a high forehead stood flat-footed at the side of the desk and a few feet away from it. A .38 caliber revolver dangled from his right hand, and a thin wisp of smoke still drifted upward from the muzzle. He frowned at Shayne and said in a perfectly reasonable voice:

"You didn't have to break the door in. I would have unlocked it after I killed the son-of-a-bitch."

Jove Books by Brett Halliday

FIT TO KILL
DIE LIKE A DOG
DOLLS ARE DEADLY
MURDER IS MY BUSINESS
BODIES ARE WHERE YOU FIND THEM
SHOOT TO KILL

SHOOT TO KILL

BRETT HALLIDAY

EISENHOWER PUBLIC
LIBRARY DISTRICT
4652 N. OLCOTT
HARWOOD HTS., IL 60656

JOVE BOOKS, NEW YORK

This Jove book contains the complete
text of the original edition.

SHOOT TO KILL

A Jove Book / published by arrangement with
Mary Dresser and Helen McCloy Dresser

PRINTING HISTORY
One previous Dell edition
New Dell edition / July 1972
Jove edition / November 1989

All rights reserved.
Copyright © 1964 by Brett Halliday.
This book may not be reproduced in whole or in part,
by mimeograph or any other means, without permission.
For information address: The Berkley Publishing Group,
200 Madison Avenue, New York, New York 10016.

ISBN: 0-515-10177-X

Jove Books are published by The Berkley Publishing Group,
200 Madison Avenue, New York, New York 10016.
The name "JOVE" and the "J" logo
are trademarks belonging to Jove Publications, Inc.

PRINTED IN THE UNITED STATES OF AMERICA

10 9 8 7 6 5 4 3 2 1

1

MICHAEL SHAYNE SAID, "NO," FLATLY AND WITHOUT emphasis, but with utter finality. He rumpled his red hair with the knobby fingers of his left hand and looked almost wonderingly across the scarred table at his oldest and closest friend in Miami. "For God's sake, Tim," he went on in a voice that patently strove to be reasonable, "I'm not a psychiatrist or marriage counsellor."

"I know," said Timothy Rourke bitterly. "You're a detective and you get paid for solving murders, so why should you be interested in preventing one? But goddamn it, Mike, I wish you'd listen to me. After Ralph spilled his guts to me last night I'm going to feel responsible if I don't do *something*."

"You do the something," said Shayne, keeping his voice indulgent and reasonable. "It certainly is none of my affair." He leaned back in the booth at the rear of Joe's Bar and lifted the sidecar in front of him and took an appreciative sip.

"It's anybody's affair," argued Rourke harshly. "If you see a guy headed for the edge of a precipice you do what you can to prevent it. Even a cynical, hard-boiled, red-headed bastard such as Mike Shayne likes to pretend to be doesn't turn his head and look the other way while the guy goes over. You at least shout out a warning to him."

"All right," said Shayne agreeably. "You see your friend Ralph Larson headed hell-bent for murder and you shout out a warning to him. I gather you did that last night. If he's too stupid to pay any attention to you, what can I do abut it?"

"I just got through telling you. Go see his wife and talk to her like a Dutch Uncle. She's the key to the whole affair. She's the stupid one. If she could just get it through her silly head that she's driving her husband straight to murder, she'd drop the whole thing like a hot tomato. Damn it, Mike, they had a good marriage until Ralph went to work for Wesley Ames and she became involved with him. I was best man at their wedding just three years ago."

"Then you're the one to talk to her like a Dutch Uncle," Shayne argued amiably. "I'm an outsider. Why should she listen to me?"

"Because you are an outsider. That would frighten her, Mike. Don't tell her I sent you. Leave me out of it altogether. You're well enough known here in town that just your name will scare hell out of her. Tell her anything. That Mrs. Ames has hired you to spy on her husband and to break up the affair he's having with Dorothy. You don't have to bring Ralph into it at all if you think it's best not to. Just go see her and play it by ear. Convince her that all hell is going to break loose if she doesn't quit seeing Wesley Ames."

"You don't know that she is seeing him. The way you just told it to me, her husband merely has these suspicions. She hasn't admitted it to him, has she?"

"I guess not. I don't think he's even accused her. Ralph was pretty drunk last night and practically incoherent, but he's absolutely convinced in his own mind that Wesley Ames is making a big play for his wife and that she's flattered by his attentions and is reciprocating. He doesn't know whether they've actually slept together or not, and that's driving him nuts. He's still crazy in love with Dorothy, and that makes him crazy jealous."

Shayne said, "Nuts," disgustedly, and emptied his sidecar glass. "You know what I think about jealous husbands who go out and kill men for making passes at their wives. No woman is worth that. Why doesn't your friend just walk away from her and let her play her extra-marital games?"

"Because he's young and he's in love," grated Rourke angrily. He lifted his highball glass with both hands and sucked at the contents greedily. "You can sit back and philosophize about the situation all you want to, Mike, but that's not going to change the basic facts. Here are two inherently decent young people who are caught up in a mess that's going to eventuate in murder unless something is done to prevent it. It's that simple." He turned his head to look over the back of the booth and catch the waiter's eye. He held up two fingers, and turned back to light a cigarette.

"Wesley Ames is a smart operator," he said bitterly. "He's a dyed-in-the-wool son-of-a-bitch, but he's suave and he's got charm and an unlimited expense account. His gossip column is syndicated in forty newspapers, and all over the country people turn to it avidly to pick up the latest dirt on celebrities cavorting at Miami's swanky night spots. All he has to do, reputedly, is crook his finger and half the society dames in the country are eager to crawl into bed with him. So if he crooks that same finger at a simple little reporter's wife like Dorothy Larson, what do you think she's going to do about it?"

The waiter brought fresh drinks and set them in front of the two men. Shayne leaned back and frowned and shook his red head in puzzlement. "On the other hand, why should he bother?"

"To crook his finger at Dorothy?"

"Yeh. If he's got all these other dames on his string."

"In the first place because Dorothy has got what it takes . . . as you'll note for yourself when you see her. She's a beautiful kid, and she's stacked. On top of that there's an aura of innocence about her that would appeal to a degenerate bastard like Ames. Besides, Ralph is obviously and helplessly in love with her. He first took on this outside job as legman for Ames in order to earn extra money to spend on Dorothy and keep her happy. That would probably be an added incentive for Ames to make a play for her. Sort of turning the screw on a poor devil who's more or less dependent on his bounty. Who knows what motivates a man like Wesley Ames?"

"You make him sound like a guy who thoroughly deserves killing."

"Hell, he deserves it all right. If society were properly arranged, the man who knocked off Ames would get a medal instead of the chair. But society isn't that far advanced, and that's why Ralph has to be stopped before this thing goes any further."

"Why not put it straight to Ames himself?" suggested Shayne easily. "That seems a lot more sensible than approaching Mrs. Larson. After all, Ames has more to lose."

"He'd laugh in your face," grated Timothy Rourke. "It would probably please his ego tremendously. No. There's only one thing to do in this situation, Mike. Make Dorothy Larson realize that she's not playing with fire, but with an atomic explosion. You don't know Ralph, and you didn't listen to him raving last night. I did. And, goddamn it, I like the guy. I'd love to see Ames dead, but I don't want Ralph to go to the chair for it. I'm putting this to you as a personal favor, Mike. Talk to Dorothy at least. Make her realize the seriousness of the situation. One of the things Ralph kept drunkenly coming back to last night is that he has a two-week vacation coming up and Dorothy wants him to go off on his own while she stays here. He's convinced in his own mind that she wants him out of the way so she can shack up with Ames while he's gone. Maybe she has got some such idea. I don't know. But I don't believe she wants both Ames and her husband dead, and I think she'd come to her senses if it were put to her that way. And you're the guy to do it, Mike. You've got no axe to grind. She won't suspect that Ralph put you up to it . . . the way she would if I went to her."

Shayne shook his head morosely. "I'll repeat what I said in the beginning. I'm not a psychiatrist or marriage counsellor. Get her minister or her priest to talk to her. It's not my responsibility."

"But it is, Mike," Rourke insisted intensely. "You're licensed as a private detective by the state of Florida and you swore an oath to uphold the due processes of the law. You're like a cop in that respect. It's a cop's job to prevent crime."

"Then let the cops do it," snarled Shayne. "Why don't you tell your story to Will Gentry and get him to go around and talk some sense into the lady? Or put Ralph Larson under arrest and hold him in protective custody? Or assign a bodyguard to Wesley Ames? Hell's bells, Tim! There are a dozen better ways to handle it than the one you suggest."

Rourke let his thin frame sink back in a slumped position against the back of the wooden bench with his head sunk down between jutting shoulder blades. He shook his head slowly and said, "You're talking through your hat, Mike, and you know you are. This thing with Ralph has got beyond routine police procedure. None of those stopgaps you mention would be any good. The only thing that will possibly work is to throw the fear of God into Dorothy Larson and bring her back to her senses. She's a good kid, Mike. Basically, she's fine. I *know* her, goddamn it. She and Ralph have got off the track somehow. It isn't for you or me to sit in judgment. You can't just sit back and complacently wash your hands of the whole affair and say they've brought it on themselves. Sure, they have. Does that mean they don't deserve help? Who the hell are you to sit back and refuse to lift a hand when it may mean life or death to a couple of intrinsically decent young people. You're not *that* cynical, Mike." The reporter's deep-set eyes blazed across the barroom table at his old friend, and his voice shook with fervor.

Shayne dropped his gaze from Rourke's and lifted his glass and drank from it deeply. He sat it down in front of him and turned it round and round with his fingers while he scowled deeply. Without lifting his eyes to meet Rourke's, he muttered, "All right. I guess I'm not. Just what the hell do you want me to do?"

"Just what I said in the beginning." Timothy Rourke was very careful not to let a tinge of triumph sound in his voice, though he could not restrain a note of relief. "Go and see Dorothy Larson. Right away. Now. After listening to Ralph rave last night, I don't think there's any time to spare. As I said before: Get tough with Dorothy. Scare the pants off her. Send her off on Ralph's vacation with him next week . . . and I'll go to work on Ralph tonight. He's got to quit his goddamned job with Ames. Running around the night spots and snooping out dirt for his filthy column is no job for a self-respecting newspaperman anyhow. Tell Dorothy that pressure is being put on Ralph to quit. They don't need that extra money. They've got to get out of the whole Ames' orbit."

"Suppose she won't see me?" muttered Shayne. "Why should she? How can I explain . . . ?"

"Oh, for Christ's sake!" exclaimed Rourke in exasperation. "You're a detective, aren't you? For more years than I like to remember you've been solving cases by barging in on people who had no desire to talk to you. Now, you ask me. Tell her any damn thing. Except that you're a friend of her husband's and feel sorry for him. Somehow, I don't think that's the right approach."

Shayne nodded his head thoughtfully, draining the last of his cocktail from the glass. "How much am I supposed to know? That is . . . what sort of games *have* she and Wesley Ames been playing? If I claim to have been hired by Mrs. Ames, for instance . . . what sort of dope am I supposed to have gathered on the two of them?"

Rourke hesitated before replying, getting his underlip between his teeth and gnawing on it indecisively. "You've sort of got me there," he confessed. "Ralph wasn't making too much sense last night. I gather that it all started a couple of months ago when Ames suggested that Ralph take Dorothy along to a couple of night spots where Ames joined them with some other doll he had in tow. Dorothy being a sort of protective coloration in making it a foursome. Then Ames apparently asked Dorothy out on a couple of occasions while Ralph was carefully sent some other place to do errands for Ames . . . all perfectly innocent, perhaps, but Ralph began adding two and two together and is now convinced that Ames is using his position as boss to keep him in some other part of town while laying his wife . . . or trying to lay her . . . Ralph isn't quite sure which it is at this point."

"Then I don't have any chapters or verses to quote to her," muttered Shayne. "No specific instances to throw in her face if she denies everything and tells me to get the hell out."

"N-no," conceded Rourke reluctantly. "I don't think Ralph has any real evidence of anything wrong. As I said before, you'll just have to play it by ear and pretend you know a lot more than you do. But she must have certain guilt feelings no matter how far she has or hasn't gone, and just having a detective show up on her doorstep at all should scare hell out of her."

"It sounds," said Shayne, "like a pretty lousy assignment. All right. Just where is her doorstep?"

"They have an apartment in the Northeast section." Rourke eagerly dug into the right-hand pocket of his baggy jacket and withdrew a folded sheet of paper. "I wrote it down for you." He unfolded it and glanced at the penciled notation, passed it across to the redhead. "Northeast Sixty-First. Right now would be a good time to walk in on her. Ralph will be tied up at the newspaper office until seven."

Shayne frowned and looked at his watch, shaking his head. "Not tonight. I've got a date to pick Lucy up at her apartment in half an hour and take her to dinner at Lucio's. Tomorrow will be soon enough for Dorothy Larson."

"Don't put it off, Mike," Rourke urged him. "I swear to God I'm afraid one more night may be one too many. Go out and see her now. I'll pick up Lucy and take her out to Lucio's. Meet us there whenever you're through with Dorothy. I'll ply Lucy with drinks and keep her happy."

"And explain that I've stood her up for another woman . . . and a well-stacked one at that?" Shayne lifted a quizzical red eyebrow at his old friend across the table.

Rourke grinned back at him and said happily, "I'll tell Lucy the truth. That you're mounted on your white charger and doing your Boy Scout good turn for the day. Get going, damn it. I'll even pay for Lucy's drinks *and* for both your dinners."

2

DRIVING OUT THROUGH THE SOFT MIAMI TWILIGHT toward the Northeast section of the city, Shayne became more and more irritated with himself for allowing Tim Rourke to talk him into undertaking this errand. It just didn't make sense to barge in on strangers and start arranging their lives for them. They were bound to resent his officious interference . . . and rightly.

And there wasn't one chance in a thousand that it would do any good. If a young couple decided to go to hell on a hay-rack, that's damn well what they were going to do, and no well-meaning advice from an outsider was likely to have the slightest effect.

Besides all that, the redheaded detective's years of experience told him that men who were really worked up by a jealous rage to the point of murder didn't talk about it beforehand. Getting drunk and making violent threats was a good way of blowing off steam, and was more likely to prevent a murder than lead up to one.

Well, he'd see Dorothy Larson and draw his own conclusions. Later on it might be worthwhile to have a talk with her husband despite Rourke's objections. That would depend a lot on Dorothy and how she reacted to his visit.

In this section of the city many small modern apartment buildings had recently been erected in blocks that had formerly been given over to moderate-priced, single-family homes, most of which had been built in the early twenties.

The address Rourke had given him proved to be one of those newer buildings. It was a square two-story structure on a large corner lot, set well in from the street on two sides behind a wide expanse of neatly-clipped lawn. There were wide concrete walks leading in to two entrances, and there were old shade trees lining the sidewalks, and scrubbed-faced, neatly-dressed children playing decorously on the lawn.

The cars parked in front of the building were uniformly gleaming late models in the medium-priced field, and Shayne maneuvered into a parking place between two of them with an increasing feeling of being an intruder in a setting specifically designed for quiet and comfortable living by middle-class people who normally lived out the full span of their lives untouched by violence or by tragedy.

He went up the walk toward the arched side entrance and found a row of mailboxes outside of wide double glass doors that stood invitingly open to a corridor carpeted from wall-to-wall and leading to a wide, curving stairway at the end.

The number under the Larson mail-box was 3-B. He could see no button to push, so Shayne went through the open doors and saw that the first apartments on either side were numbered 1-A and 2-A. He continued past 3-A and 4-A, and climbed the stairs and found 3-B on his right at the top. The door was closed, but the door directly across the hall stood half open and the muted sound of music came through it. That was the only sound to be heard as he pressed the button beside the closed door of 3-B. He took his hat off as he waited, and got a pleasant smile ready, and wondered what the devil he was going to say to Mrs. Larson when she opened the door.

He waited a full minute without hearing any sound from within the apartment, and was lifting his hand to press the button again when a pleasant voice spoke from behind him, "The Larsons aren't home if that's who you're looking for."

Shayne turned his head and saw that the door of 4-B now stood wide open and the tall figure of a woman was framed in the opening.

She was in her late thirties and she was bare-footed and bare-legged. She wore a short, peasant skirt of bright green cotton material that came just to her knees and a tight yellow blouse of sheer silk that showed the full contours of unbrassiered breasts even at that distance. She also wore a plenitude of crimson lipstick on her wide, full-lipped mouth, and an open, welcoming smile on her face. Her voice was throaty and warm, and it was welcoming too in a cheerful woman-to-man sort of way, so that it managed to be inviting without being brazen.

The smile Michael Shayne had prepared for Dorothy Larson came easily to his rugged face in response to hers, and he turned slowly, asking, "Do you have any idea when they'll be home?"

"He's never in till late ... midnight or after." She leaned her left shoulder comfortably against the door frame and rested her right hand lazily on her hip. "But if it's Dottie you want, I expect she'll be coming along any minute." She paused, appraising him openly with eyes which narrowed a trifle and made pleasant crinkles at the corners, letting him sense that she liked what she saw. "You could wait in here if you like."

Shayne said, "I would like."

She did not stir from her stance in the doorway as

he took two steps across the hall toward her. He stopped a foot in front of her and she straightened up and dropped her arm to her side, and in her bare feet her eyes were not more than three inches below the level of his own. He could smell whiskey on her breath, and there was the bold darkness of nipples behind the sheer yellow fabric of her blouse.

Studying his face quizzically, she worked her full crimson lips as though she were tasting something good, and she tilted her head slightly and asked, "What would you like, Red?"

Then she laughed quickly and happily, very much like a little girl's laugh, and she linked her left arm in his and turned and drew him inside the apartment, and said gaily, "Don't answer that. You came to see Dottie. But I will give you a drink on account of I want another one myself and I make it a strict rule never to drink alone . . . that is if there's anyone else around to drink with. So, what'll you have, Red?" She released his arm from hers and turned her back and padded toward the kitchen in her bare feet, moving hips and shoulders sinuously, and Shayne called after her, "Anything. Brandy if you happen to have it."

She disappeared through the open doorway and her voice floated back with a trace of indignation in it, "Of course there's brandy . . . if I can find it. Rest your feet while I dig it out."

Shayne found himself grinning appreciatively after her as he stood there in the center of her living room, and he hoped Dorothy Larson wouldn't show up too soon.

He got out a cigarette and lit it, and looked around him slowly. It was a pleasantly furnished and comfortably cluttered, feminine-looking room. The long sofa along one wall was covered with gold brocade and littered with small soft cushions in bright contrasting colors that managed not to clash. There were end tables with big utilitarian ashtrays on them, and two comfortable-looking overstuffed chairs ranged against the wall opposite the sofa. The muted music he had heard through the door was coming from a stereo set with twin speakers that were detached from it and set at right angles in different corners of the room. The music was not familiar to him, classical, he thought, probably one of the three B's. A door at the end of the room directly in front of him opened onto a bedroom with a big double bed that was unmade and had two rumpled pillows at the head of it.

Shayne liked everything he saw as he stood there and heard clinking sounds of glass against glass in the kitchen, and he frowned and tried to analyze the warm feeling of contentment that welled up inside him. It was definitely a woman's place, and yet it welcomed his masculinity and made him feel immediately wanted. He did not know why that was, or how the woman in the kitchen had managed it so well, but he did know instinctively that she had managed it, not consciously probably, but as an expression of herself.

He went to one of the deep chairs and sat down as she came back into the room carrying a glass in each hand. In her right hand was a big, bulbous brandy snifter with at least four ounces of amber fluid in the bottom of it. The other glass was tall, with tinkling ice cubes submerged in a dark brown mixture which appeared to be about three-quarters bourbon and one-quarter water.

She stopped in front of him and extended the snifter, frowning anxiously. "It says Napoleon

V.O.P. on the bottle, and it smells okay. If you'd rather have something else . . . ?"

Shayne took the big glass and inhaled the fragrance and assured her, "This is wonderful."

She turned across the room from him and curled up on the sofa with her bare feet under her and took a long, sturdy drink from her own glass. She blew out her breath strongly and looked over her shoulder at the open door into the corridor, and said, "We leave it open, huh? So you'll know when Dottie comes."

Shayne shrugged and said evenly, "I do want to see her. In the meantime . . ." He lifted his glass and looked across the room at her over the top of it. ". . . here's to you." He tilted the glass and drank deeply.

She was looking at him with her eyes wide and probing as he set the glass down on the table beside his chair with a happy sigh. "You've got me puzzled, Red. I can't figure you out. You and Dottie . . . ?" She paused, delicately. Speculatively.

"Do you know her well?"

"Dottie? We've been next door neighbors for three months. You a friend of that squirt of a husband of hers?"

"Ralph?" Shayne shook his head. "I never met him." He paused and added deliberately, "I understand he's the jealous type."

"Of her?" She widened her eyes and leaned back against the sofa, stretching her bare legs out in front of her languidly, clasping both hands behind her neck and thrusting her torso upward so that upthrust nipples were clearly and provocatively defined, and her steady, wide-eyed gaze challenged him to ignore them . . . to ignore her . . . to be unaware of the whole hunk of lush femininity she was flaunting in front of him.

She said throatily, "I wouldn't know, Red. She's a lady. Dottie is. A real lady-bitch type. Different from me."

"What type are you?"

"I'm a woman, Red. Like you don't know." She relaxed and sat upright and grinned suddenly. A gamin-like grin. "Like you didn't know the moment you turned your head and looked at me across the hall. Like any real man knows when he looks at a real woman." She laced her fingers in front of her face and peered through the interstices at him and said wonderingly in a low voice that was throaty with desire, "You could close that damned door and lock it, Red. Then you could kiss me."

She was a lot drunker than he had thought, Shayne realized, and he was sorry. He wished to God he were a lot drunker . . . or she were soberer. Either way. . . .

He fumbled for his glass and picked it up and glared at it, then put it up to his mouth and drained the remaining three ounces of liquor out of it.

He got up out of his chair then, and moved a step toward her, and stopped when he saw her eyes were open. She was watching him, and waiting.

He forced a grin onto his face and ran both hands through his rumpled red hair. He said, "This is a hell of a time. . . ."

"I know." She lay on her side on the sofa, staring up at him unblinkingly. "You're like me, Red." She sounded sad. Desolated and torn. He wondered if she was really as drunk as he had thought her to be. She smiled slowly. A crooked, understanding sort of smile. She said, "We're two of a kind. Ships that pass in the night. But we'll meet again, Red. Next time, we won't pass." She shuddered violently and closed her eyes and was silent.

Shayne didn't realize he had moved, but suddenly he was standing close beside the sofa and was looking down at her. She kept her eyes tightly closed, but he knew that she knew he stood there, and he hesitated, clenching his fists tightly together so his fingernails bit into the flesh of his palms.

Then, through the open door behind him he heard the light clickity-clack of high heels mounting the uncarpeted stairs toward the second floor. He turned his head, still standing close beside the sofa, dropping his left hand toward the woman who lay curled up there, feeling her fingers twist around his, tightly, warmly, compellingly.

Through the open door at his right he saw a slender, smartly-clad young woman reach the top of the stairs and turn toward the door opposite him with a key held in her outthrust hand.

She was well-stacked, as Timothy Rourke had told him. She was also beautiful, with a careful precision of features that made her into a "real lady-bitch type."

She unlocked the door of Apartment 3-B and walked inside without bothering to glance over her shoulder at the open door of 4-B.

Shayne stood unmoving until she closed the door behind her. His left hand was still tightly gripped by the woman who lay on the sofa with her eyes closed.

He turned to look down at her, and he lightly said, "Hi."

She opened her eyes and smiled up at him. "You didn't close the door did you, Red?"

He shook his head from side to side. "Next time, I will."

She said, "Okay. Next time." Her fingers released his, and she closed her eyes again.

Shayne walked out of her apartment and crossed the hall and put his finger on the electric button beside the Larsons' door.

3

THE DOOR OPENED ALMOST IMMEDIATELY AND DOROTHY Larson stood in front of him, a frown slowly forming on her beautifully chiseled features as she looked him up and down.

Shayne had his smile all ready to put on, but he abruptly decided not to waste it on her. He made his voice impersonal and somewhat harsh as he said, "Mrs. Ralph Larson?"

"Yes. I'm Mrs. Larson. What do you want?" Her voice was as chilly as the cold, cornflower blue of her eyes.

"To talk to you a minute."

She said, "I'm sorry, Mister, but I practically never talk to strange men who come ringing my doorbell." She took a backward step and firmly started to close the door in his face.

Shayne had his big shoe in the way and the door stayed open a couple of feet. He said, "You'll talk to me no matter what you practically never do. About Wesley Ames." He put his hand on the doorknob and pushed it open against her effort to hold it shut.

She retreated three steps away from him into the room and said coldly, "If you don't get out this instant I shall call the police."

Shayne said, "I'm a detective, Mrs. Larson." He had no difficulty making his tone match hers.

"A detective? What on earth do you want? What about Mr. Ames?"

"About you and Mr. Ames," amplified Shayne. "About the affair you and he are carrying on."

"What has a *detective* to do with my private affairs?"

"Well, you see I'm a private detective," Shayne told her stolidly. "My name is Michael Shayne," he added. "Make up your mind fast. Do you want to talk to me or shall I go to your husband?"

"Ralph would laugh in your face. He works for Mr. Ames." She lifted her chin disdainfully.

"I don't think Ralph would laugh in my face. In fact, I'm quite certain he wouldn't laugh at all. And so are you," he added harshly. "You know the poor guy is crazy in love with you. What you don't know, evidently, is that he isn't as dumb as you think. If he gets my report there's going to be hell to pay, Mrs. Larson."

"Your . . . report?" she gasped. "Do you mean he's hired a detective to check up on me?"

"Did you think you had the wool pulled completely over his eyes?" Shayne quibbled. He folded his arms across his chest and sneered at her, and somehow found himself enjoying it.

"What do you want from me?" she demanded. "Do you think I'll pay you blackmail?"

"No goddamnit," said Shayne savagely. "I'm not here to blackmail you. I'm here to talk some sense into your silly head. Contrary to a great many popular misconceptions, all private detectives aren't crooks and double-crossers. I happen to like your husband. I think he's a decent guy and I feel sorry as hell for him married to a woman like you. I'm offering you a chance to come to your senses and break off with Ames before Ralph finds out the truth and kills himself or you or Ames . . . or all three of you. Maybe you don't love the guy," he went on harshly. "But you don't want to see him in the electric chair, do you?"

"No," she cried thinly. "Oh God, *no*. I never thought. . . ." She put her hands up to her face suddenly and began to cry.

"It's time you started thinking," Shayne told her. "I happen to know Ralph has a vacation next week and he suspects the reason you want him to go off on his own while you stay in Miami alone is so you can be with Ames."

"That isn't true," she cried wildly. "I just need time to be alone and think."

"Whether it's true or not," Shayne told her brutally, "Ralph thinks it is. And if I make my report to him he's going to be sure of it. And just as sure as God made little apples he's going to go gunning for Wesley Ames and there'll be all hell to pay."

"You can't have anything . . . really bad to tell him." She was getting her sobbing under control and she lifted a stricken, tear-streaked face to Shayne. "It isn't as though . . . Wesley and I haven't. . . ."

"I've got enough of a dossier on the two of you to send a man like your husband off his rocker," Shayne lied harshly and convincingly.

She didn't attempt to deny it. She asked weakly, "What do you want me to do? If he finds out you've been here. . . ."

"Don't admit you've ever seen me," Shayne told her promptly. "This is completely unethical on my part, but in this case I think the end justifies the means. Don't let Ralph even suspect that you know about him putting a private detective on your trail. That would ruin everything. You've got to make him think you've come to your senses all on your own and are sorry you ever met Wesley Ames. Insist on going off on vacation with him, and urge him to quit this side job he's doing for Ames. He's a good newspaper reporter and he can earn enough on his job to support you.

"Maybe you're not really in love with him," Shayne went on swiftly, glad that Timothy Rourke couldn't hear him now because by God he was beginning to sound like a marriage counsellor. "Maybe you should separate. But let that come later. Your job right now is to convince your husband that you're in love with him and that your playing around with Wesley Ames has been completely innocent."

"And if I do that, you'll . . . you're willing to doctor your report so he'll never know the truth?" she asked slowly.

"I give you my word," said Shayne honestly, "that he'll never learn differently from me. But it has to be tonight," he warned her sternly. "As soon as he gets home. Don't put it off because I can't stall him very long. Call me on the telephone first thing in the morning and tell me it's done," he directed her. "Get a pencil and write down my telephone number."

He waited while she turned away meekly and went to the telephone stand and got a pad and a pencil. He gave her his hotel number and she wrote it down.

"That's my home number," he explained. "You can reach me there until nine or ten tomorrow morning. After that, call my office." He gave her that number.

"If I don't hear from you by noon tomorrow it will be too late," he told her. "Don't forget that you'll be responsible for whatever happens."

She nodded and hung her head and said, "I guess I've been an awful damn fool, Mike Shayne. I've changed my mind about private detectives."

"Most of us are damn fools at times," Shayne assured her. "And stop watching the private eye shows on television. Just because a man is a licensed private investigator it doesn't make him into a complete heel." He stopped, grinning at himself as he realized that he was beginning to sound positively mawkish.

"All right," he said briskly. "So much for that. My Boy Scout deed is accomplished. I'll now dismount from my white charger and go find some more keyholes to peek through." He turned away from her and opened the door and went out and closed it firmly behind him.

He was feeling good, by God. Surprisingly good. Despite his cynical scoffing at Timothy Rourke earlier he was glad he had come.

He'd ended up almost liking Dorothy, and he was feeling very smug and paternal about the whole thing.

He noted that the door of 4-B was now tightly closed as he hesitated there in the corridor. At the moment he didn't know whether he was sorry or glad. She was quite a person . . . that barefooted one. And she served good brandy. What the devil *was* Napoleon V.O.P.? It was a new one on him. He wondered if she had made it up, and he suspected that she had.

Ships that pass in the night!

Next time he would close the door and lock it.

But right now Tim Rourke and his brown-haired secretary were waiting for him at Lucio's, and Tim was going to pay for the drinks *and* dinner, and he and Lucy were both going to be properly impressed when he related the manner in which he had handled the Dorothy Larson affair.

He stopped at the row of mail-boxes outside the open glass doors and looked at 4-B.

"May Graham."

He liked that. Not Mr. and Mrs. Not Mrs. Graham. Just May.

Somehow that was right for a big, barefooted woman who called him Red without waiting for an introduction.

Michael Shayne felt very much at peace with the world as he went down the walk to his parked car.

4

LUCIO HIMSELF MET THE REDHEAD AT THE ARCHED doorway of the pleasant dining room overlooking Biscayne Bay. He said happily, "Your friends are already here, Mr. Shayne. I have put them at a nice table in the corner." He led the way through the uncrowded room and Shayne saw Timothy Rourke and Lucy Hamilton seated across from each other at a round table in front of a window that showed the lights of Miami Beach gleaming through the early darkness along the peninsula that formed the eastern shore of the bay.

Lucy had a champagne cocktail in front of her and was leaning forward across the table talking animatedly to the reporter who was slumped back in his customary pose and nodding slowly with an intent expression on his face.

Soft overhead light glinted on her brown hair, bringing out a faintly reddish tinge which blended nicely with the smooth tan of her face and shoulders which was accentuated by the low-cut white gown she wore, and Shayne slowed down behind Lucio as he neared the table to enjoy another moment of looking at Lucy before she was aware of his presence.

The picture of May Graham came fleetingly to his mind by way of sharp contrast, and he was glad, now, that her door had been shut when he let himself out of the Larson apartment. Men were inherently lecherous bastards, he told himself with a trace of self-anger and more than a trace of self-guilt. Let a woman like May flaunt her sex in front of him and he started braying like a jackass at stud. When all the time there was a charming, sweet, intelligent girl like Lucy Hamilton waiting patiently in the background. . . .

He stopped beside the table as Lucio drew out a chair, and looked down into Lucy's sparkling brown eyes when she glanced up at him, and she was startled for a moment by the intensity of his expression. Her bright smile faded and she exclaimed, "Michael! You look as though you'd never seen me before."

"I've never seen you look so devastating," he told her. "How many champagne cocktails have you had?"

"This is just my second, but I'll certainly have several more if they're going to produce that effect on my boss."

Shayne nodded approvingly and said, "You do that. Tim's paying the bill tonight. Did you hear that, Lucio?" he added to the proprietor as he seated himself between the two.

"Assuredly, Mr. Shayne. A sidecar for you? With Martel and not too heavy on the cointreau, eh?"

Shayne said, "Please," and Rourke leaned toward him eagerly and asked, "Did you see the lady, Mike?"

"I saw her."

"And talked to her?"

"Like a Dutch Uncle."

"And did you . . . ?"

"I scared the pants off her." Shayne glanced at Lucy and grinned. "Don't take that literally, angel. I don't even know whether she had any pants on. Anyhow, she promised to start behaving herself like a proper wife and quit seeing Wesley Ames. I don't know how much Tim told you about this, Lucy. . . ."

"He told me all about it." She screwed up her face in a grimace of distaste and then drank from her tall-stemmed glass. "From what I've heard of Wesley Ames I'm not at all certain that you did humanity any great favor by persuading Tim's friend not to kill him."

"I'm sure it's only a temporary reprieve," Rourke assured her. "There must be dozens of people gunning for Ames and one of them will certainly catch up with him before long. I'll just be happy if it isn't Ralph Larson. How did Dorothy react, Mike?"

A brimming sidecar was placed in front of Shayne by their waiter. He lifted it carefully so as not to spill a single drop and drank half of it with open pleasure.

"She indignantly denied any wrong-doing with Ames, but she somehow got the impression that her husband had hired me to get the dirt on the two of them, and she certainly wasn't anxious to have me tell him what I'd found out." He shrugged and took another sip of his cocktail. "I'd say she's basically a cold and calculating type."

"But 'damn well-stacked' according to Tim's graphic description," gurgled Lucy.

Shayne said disparagingly, "Any woman who can fill a B-cup is well-stacked according to Tim. And that reminds me . . . have you ever seen the Larsons' neighbor from across the hall, Tim?"

"*What* reminds you?" demanded Lucy.

"Not B-cups," Shayne assured her with a sidelong, teasing grin. "How about it, Tim?"

"I've never been to that apartment. But I do believe I've heard a description of the lady's charms from Ralph soon after they moved in. Magnified in the telling, no doubt."

Shayne chuckled and said, "That I doubt." He

glanced at Lucy and saw a frosty look of suspicion beginning to dawn on her face, and explained hastily, "She's one of those females who goes slopping around in the afternoon barefooted, angel. Not my type at all."

"You seem to have done a fair amount of detecting in a rather short time," she suggested.

"Not really. I just happened to catch a glimpse of her while I was ringing the Larson doorbell. What's the most expensive thing on the menu?" Shayne picked it up and spread it out in front of him, hiding his face behind it while he ostentatiously ran a blunt forefinger down the list of prices at the right-hand side.

It was just seven-thirty when the trio left the restaurant after an excellent dinner over which they had dawdled comfortably and companionably and for which Timothy Rourke had paid the bill without protest.

As they went out into the warm night, Shayne suggested, "Suppose Lucy and I go along to her apartment and you follow us, Tim, and stop for a nightcap. You don't need to get back to the paper for another hour, do you?"

"No, but my car's there now," Rourke told him. "I picked Lucy up in a taxi because I knew you were meeting us here."

"Then we'll all go to Lucy's together," Shayne decided. "I'll take you on to the office whenever you want because I'm headed for an early bed and a solid night's sleep."

Timothy Rourke said sure, that would be fine with him, and they all got in the front seat of Shayne's car and he drove back to Biscayne Boulevard and turned south toward the city.

They were a few blocks from Lucy's turnoff when

she wriggled uncomfortably on the seat between them and said plaintively, "Michael. I've just remembered something terrible. You're going to beat me for sure."

"What's terrible?" he asked indulgently.

"I haven't got any cognac," she confessed in a stricken voice. "Remember? Last time you were there you finished the bottle."

"But that was over a week ago," he protested. "You've had plenty of time to pick up another one."

"I know. And the last time I ran out you threatened to beat me if I ever let it happen again. And I forgot."

"With a cat-o-nine-tails," Shayne amplified with relish. "You're a witness, Tim. These damn secretaries. Won't even go to the trouble of stocking their boss's favorite beverage on the chance that he may drop in for a drink. All right for you, young lady." He kept on driving steadily south, passing the street on which Lucy lived. "We'll all go to my place where there *is* cognac. And we'll have a drink or two or three and I'll work myself up into the proper mood and then I'll flog you, but good. While Tim holds you firmly over his knees."

"Just so there's bourbon as well as cognac," Rourke said firmly. "Last time I was up at your room I had to make do with Scotch."

"An entire fifth, if my memory serves," Shayne agreed drily. "I assure you I hurried out the next day and stocked up with cheap bourbon. Your favorite. Old Outhouse."

Rourke said, "Ah," fondly, and smacked his lips in anticipation, and Lucy giggled and Shayne slowed for the traffic light at Flagler Street and then drove on and made a right turn and a left turn to draw into the curb at the side entrance to his hotel on the north bank of the Miami River where he had maintained a second-floor bachelor apartment since either of them had known him.

They got out and went in a side door and up a single flight of stairs that by-passed the lobby, and past the elevators to a door which opened into the shabby suite which both his visitors knew so well.

Entering in front of them, Shayne switched on the ceiling light with a wall switch and tossed his hat on a rack beside the door in passing. He headed straight for the kitchen on the right, saying, "Set out the bottles, Tim, and I'll get a pitcher of ice. You want Benedictine to settle those champagne cocktails, Lucy?"

"I don't want to *settle* them," she protested. "What a horrible thought! Can't I have a C and C instead?"

"Now what in hell," asked Rourke wonderingly, "is a C and C? I've heard of B and B's, but . . ."

"A C and C is Michael's own private receipt . . . for a sidecar when he hasn't any lemons. And he never does."

"Cognac and cointreau," guessed Rourke, going toward the liquor cabinet on the wall near the kitchen door. "So that's what he plies his women with? Lucy, I would never have suspected. . . ."

The telephone on the center table in the living room interrupted him. Both he and Lucy turned to look at it accusingly. Neither of them did anything constructive and it kept on ringing until Shayne came in from the kitchen with a tray that had a pitcher of ice cubes and various sized glasses.

The telephone continued to ring while he set the tray on the table beside it. He picked it up and said, "Mike Shayne," into the mouthpiece.

A woman's voice came leaping over the wire, shrill

with fright and hysteria: "Mr. Shayne! You've got to stop Ralph. He's got a gun and he's going to kill Mr. Ames."

"Is that Mrs. Larson?"

"Yes. Of course. Didn't you hear me? Don't you understand? Ralph is like a raving maniac. He's on his way to the Ames house now. You've got to stop him."

"Have you called the police?"

"The police? No. I don't want him *arrested*. Can't you hurry and stop him?"

"Where does Ames live?"

"It's Northeast One-Hundred and Twentieth Street. Near the Bay. I don't know the street number, but. . . ."

Shayne said, "I'm on my way." He dropped the instrument on its prongs and whirled to face the other two who were standing in the center of the room looking at him with open mouths.

"Call the cops, Lucy. Emergency. Get a radio car out to the Wesley Ames residence on Northeast Hundred and Twentieth Street near the bayshore. Ralph Larson is on his way out there with a gun and he's got a hell of a head start on us. Come on, Tim."

He was trotting toward the door as he ended, and he jerked it open and went out hatless. Timothy Rourke was close behind him as he pounded down the hallway to the stairs and down to the side entrance. He ran around to the driver's seat of his parked car and the reporter slid in beside him as he turned on the ignition. He grimly made a screaming U-turn in front of oncoming traffic, made a sweeping right turn on a yellow light at the first intersection, and gunned the heavy car viciously to catch a green light at the Boulevard and straighten out northward on the long run to 120th Street.

Timothy Rourke sat tensely beside him, leaning forward with both hands clasped over his knees, his lips moving in a mumbled prayer while Shayne picked holes in the traffic, weaving from the inner lane to the center and outside, using his horn angrily and alternating with brakes and accelerator to hit the traffic lights as they changed color up the Boulevard.

"You don't *have* to get there in nothing flat," muttered Rourke plaintively. "Better if we make it all in one piece. Lucy will have called the police. If there's a patrol car cruising nearby they'll be in time to stop the fool."

"*If* there's a car close," Shayne agreed grimly. "If not he'll practically be there by this time. He was halfway there before we started."

"But he won't be making eighty through traffic the way you are. *Goddamn* it, Mike." Rourke shuddered and closed his eyes as the redhead cut in front of a car on his left and slid through a hole that should have taken the paint off both sides of his car but somehow didn't.

"Keep your eyes closed," Shayne advised him cheerfully. "That's Seventy-Ninth ahead. If I can hit that light...."

He did hit it a moment after it changed to red, but side traffic hadn't begun to move and he went through the intersection unscathed. Traffic was thinner north of Seventy-Ninth, and Rourke forced himself to relax and he asked wonderingly, "What in hell happened to trigger Ralph off tonight? I thought you had it all set with Dorothy...."

"I thought so too. She didn't say over the phone. Just that he had a gun and was on his way to kill Ames. Goddamn woman probably changed her mind," he grated. "Threw it in his face or something. Know what kind of car Ralph drives?"

"N-no. Blue with a white top, I think. One of the new compacts. I can't tell one from another."

They passed 110th Street doing eighty-five and Shayne took his foot off the gas and said, "We'll know soon enough. If the cops are already there and got him, let me handle it, Tim. Jail is the best place for him until he cools off."

He touched the accelerator lightly again to maintain a speed of forty as he approached 120th, braked sharply and swung to the right on a two-lane street that dead-ended against the western shore of Biscayne Bay a few blocks ahead. There were no taillights ahead of them. Scattered houses were lighted on either side of the street, large estates that appeared calm and peaceful at this early evening hour.

"I think it's on the end at the right." Rourke was sitting erect scanning the houses as they passed. "I was here at a party once several years ago. I remember there's a stone wall and wide entrance gates."

The last house on the right was a large mansion at the end of a short drive through an arched gateway behind a high stone wall. The driveway and a large paved parking area in front was brilliantly lighted by two glaring floodlights mounted well up at either end of the house.

Two cars were in sight as Shayne swung into the driveway. A black Cadillac sedan stood under the *porte-cochère* and a blue and white compact was parked directly behind it. Lights blazed from the lower front windows of the house, and the front door opened and the figure of a man disappeared inside and the door slammed shut just as Shayne swung in behind the compact.

He cut his motor and leaped out, and heard a loud shout and something that sounded like a crash from inside the house as he sprinted toward the front door.

It opened inward onto a large square living room that was brilliantly illuminated like a stage setting.

A man lay on his side ten feet in front of the door, struggling up to a sitting posture, his mouth ludicrously open although no words were coming out, and pointing a trembling finger toward the stairway at the rear.

A silver tray lay on the floor in front of the stairway, and there were broken glasses and bottles strewn around it. A small, white-coated figure was running up the stairs as Shayne lunged in through the front door with Rourke close behind him, and he disappeared at the top and Shayne heard a door slam loudly on the second floor.

Shayne ran toward the stairs, skirting the broken glass and bottles, and mounted as fast as he could with Rourke pounding close at his heels.

Half-way down a wide carpeted corridor at the left the white-coated man was pounding a small fist on a closed wooden door while he ineffectually twisted the knob with his other hand. A printed "Do Not Disturb" sign hung from the knob. He turned a frightened, brown, Puerto Rican face over his shoulder to look toward Shayne as the redhead reached the top of the stairs, and he jabbered something in Spanish while he continued to pound on the door.

Shayne reached him in four long strides and clamped a big hand on his shoulder to thrust him aside from the door, then drew back and lowered his shoulder to drive his weight at it.

Before he could make a lunge a muffled shot sounded beyond the closed door. Shayne hesitated momentarily and then hit the door with his shoulder.

It shuddered with the impact, but did not give a fraction of an inch.

There was silence inside the room as Shayne stepped back for another try. Somewhere down the hallway a door opened, and the Puerto Rican houseman was slumped back against the wall, his eyes wide and round and staring and his mouth making small whimpering sounds.

Shayne hit the door again with his bruised shoulder, this time lower and closer to the lock, and there was the protesting screech of screws being torn from wood and the door burst open, almost catapulting the detective forward on his face.

He caught the door-jamb and straightened himself slowly. It was a large room, fitted up as an office or study, with a big flat-topped desk set squarely in the center of it and a dead man slumped sideways, half-in and half-out of an armchair behind the desk.

A thin intense-faced young man with a lock of black hair slanted across a high forehead stood flat-footed at the side of the desk and a few feet away from it. He was in his shirtsleeves with a black tie dangling loosely. A .38 calibre revolver dangled from his right hand and a thin wisp of smoke still drifted upward from the muzzle. He frowned at Shayne in a puzzled manner and said in a perfectly reasonable voice:

"You didn't have to break the door in. I would have unlocked it after I killed the son-of-a-bitch."

Michael Shayne drew in a deep breath and expelled it slowly. He went toward the young man, holding out his hand, "Better let me have the gun."

"Sure." A twisted grin crossed Ralph Larson's face and he jerked his head to toss the lock of black hair away from his eyes. He took the barrel of the .38 in his left hand and ceremoniously offered the butt to Shayne. Then he looked past the redhead and said indifferently to Rourke, "Hello, Tim. You know I told you I was going to kill him. So I did, by God."

Timothy Rourke said tightly, "I know." He moved slowly into the room behind Shayne.

The detective slid the gun into his hip pocket and turned to look at the dead man. At that moment the wail of a police siren came to their ears. It rose to a banshee shriek as it approached the house rapidly, and then died to a low moan and silence in the driveway outside.

"He laughed at me, Tim," Ralph Larson said earnestly, as though it was terribly necessary to explain things and justify himself. "He sat right there in the goddamned chair and laughed in my face when I told him I was going to kill him. He just couldn't believe it, you see. His goddamned ego just wouldn't allow him to accept the fact that I meant what I said. He was Wesley Ames, you see. He was immune from the fate that overtakes ordinary mortals. So he didn't take me seriously. He laughed at me. Well, he knows better now. He's not laughing now, by God. Because the joke's on him. I'm the one who's doing the laughing."

And he did. He threw back his head and laughed. High, shrill laughter that cut through the silence in the room like a knife. Then he put his hands over his face and sank slowly down to sit cross-legged on the floor and his laughter turned into sobbing.

Outside the room there was the loud purposeful tramp of feet on the stairway, and voices, and Shayne turned to the open door to confront the police officers who had responded to Lucy's telephone call too late.

5

THE FIRST MAN THROUGH THE DOOR WAS BULKY AND blue-coated, with a big protruding paunch and dull-witted, porcine features. He waved a service revolver menacingly, breathing heavily through open mouth; and he narrowed close-set eyes at Rourke and at Shayne, and then at the sobbing man seated on the floor and finally at the murdered man behind the desk.

"What's going on here, huh? Stand still all of you. Nobody make a move." He swung his revolver around, pointing it at first one and then the other, pouting his thick lips and drawing himself up with an air of ponderous authority on wide-spread flat feet.

"Been a shooting, huh?" He sniffed the air with satisfaction, nodding his head slowly. Behind him a younger officer peered over his shoulder, and in the hallway behind him Shayne could see the man whom they had passed in the living room downstairs and the houseman, and another round-faced man who had appeared from nowhere. The trio were drawn together in a little knot, speaking anxiously to each other in low voices.

"Yep. Been a shooting, all right," the first officer announced with finality. "You, there!" he snarled suddenly at Michael Shayne. "What's that I see in your hip pocket?"

"It's a gun," Shayne told him quietly. He dropped

his hand to the butt of the .38 to pull it out, but the policeman shouted, "None of that. Keep your hands *up*, hear me?" He swung his revolver around so the barrel was leveled at the redhead's belly and said, "There's been enough shooting. Just keep your hands up and turn around slowly, Mister, and face the wall."

Shayne turned slowly as he was directed, and Timothy Rourke burst out impatiently, "For God's sake, Officer, that's Mike Shayne. We came here. . . ."

"I don't care if he's Jesus Christ, and I figure to find out why you came here. You just keep your mouth shut while I handle this here according to regulations. Step forward about three feet from the wall," he directed Shayne, "and lean forward and put your hands out flat so they're holding up your weight."

Shayne followed his instructions silently.

"Now then, Powers," the big cop ordered his companion with satisfaction, "you step up there and take that gun off his hip while I keep him covered."

He stepped aside and the younger man passed in front of Rourke to lift the .38 out of Shayne's pocket.

"Hand it over to me," the bulky man directed, and he took the revolver and smelled the muzzle of it and announced, "Been fired just recently all right. I guess we got the murder weapon, Powers. You better take a look at that man behind the desk," he added as an afterthought. "He looks dead enough from here, but in a case like this we got to make sure."

Shayne pushed himself up erect from his awkward position and folded his arms across his chest and watched sardonically while Powers circled the desk and knelt down to take the victim's dangling left wrist between his fingers and feel for a pulse. "He's shot right square through the middle of the chest," he announced. "There's a hole and some blood but not very much it looks like to me. He's dead all right, Griffin." He let go of the wrist and rocked back on his heels and averted his eyes from the corpse. "What do we do now?"

"What you'd damn well better do," Shayne grated savagely between his teeth, "is get down to your radio and call in to Headquarters. This is a job for Homicide and nothing should be touched in this room until they get here."

"You telling me how to handle this?" Griffin swung a broadly amazed face toward the redhead.

Shayne said, "I'm telling you. And you'd better listen if you don't want to go back to pounding a beat."

"Is that so, Mister? And just who in hell do you think you are?"

"I told you who he was," said Rourke disgustedly. "He's Mike Shayne. And I'm Rourke from the *News* for Chrissake. We're the ones who called in the report in the first place and tried to get here in time to prevent a killing."

"I think that redhead *is* Mike Shayne, Griff," said Powers anxiously. "You know, the private dick that's such good friends with Chief Gentry. We should call in to Homicide, I guess."

"I don't care whether he's a private dick or not, or who he's friends of," said Griffin ominously. "I know we got a dead man here and him with a gun that was still smoking in his pocket. Sure, go down and call in to Homicide," he decided magnanimously. "Tell 'em we got their killer rounded up and dead to rights."

The younger officer got to his feet and hurried out of the room, the three men still clustered in the doorway drawing back to let him pass.

"Now then," said Griffin importantly. "You there, sitting on the floor with your face in your hands. What do you know about this. Come on, speak up," he added impatiently as Ralph Larson took his hands from his face and looked up at him dazedly. "Were you a witness to the shooting?"

Shayne squared his wide shoulders, then stepped over beside Larson and reached down to take hold of his arm and help him stand up. "Don't answer any questions," he advised the young man. "You'll just have to repeat your answers later when Homicide gets here. All of us," he announced firmly, "should get out of this room and leave it exactly as it is. You know that much, Griffin. Quit throwing your weight around. And just so you won't look like a complete fool when Sergeant Griggs gets here to take over, this is Ralph Larson standing beside me. He's a reporter on the *News* with Tim Rourke who is standing behind me. Tim and I got here about sixty seconds too late to prevent him from shooting Wesley Ames. Two of those men in the hallway will tell you the same thing. I don't know who the other one is or how much he saw. Now, can we all go downstairs and rustle up a drink, maybe?"

"Why didn't you tell me all this in the beginning?" demanded Griffin. "How was I supposed to know . . . ?"

"You aren't supposed to know anything," Shayne told him disgustedly. "Come on Ralph, and Tim." Still holding firmly to Larson's arm he went toward the door that was sagging inward on its hinges, and Griffin moved aside uncertainly to let him pass.

In the hallway, Shayne nodded to the three

men there who had drawn back in a huddle and told them, "We should all go downstairs and wait for the arrival of the Homicide Squad. They will want statements from all of you, but in the meantime I advise you to keep quiet. Mr. Ames is dead," he went on with a shrug of his shoulders. "We can't do anything for him up here." He went toward the head of the stairs with Ralph wavering along beside him and Rourke on the other side of the reporter.

After a moment's hesitation the three men followed along behind them, and Officer Griffin appeared in the doorway of Ames' study to announce loudly, "I'll stay on guard here to see that nothing's disturbed. None of you are to leave the premises, do you understand?"

None of them bothered to reply to him as they went down the stairs. Suddenly, Michael Shayne had assumed control of the situation and was tacitly accepted as the one in authority despite his lack of uniform or badge.

Downstairs the silver tray, broken glasses and two bottles still lay on the floor where they had fallen. Shayne stopped beside them and looked down at the two corked bottles. One was Scotch and one was bourbon. The white-coated Puerto Rican knelt beside the tray and began picking up pieces of glass. Rourke went on across the room with Larson toward a settee, and the other two men hesitated at the foot of the stairs behind Shayne.

Shayne asked the houseman, "What's your name?"

"Alfred, sir."

"As soon as you pick up the bigger pieces of glass, do you suppose you could find us some fresh ones in the kitchen . . . with some ice?"

Looking past him at the two men to whom he hadn't been introduced and to whom he hadn't spoken previously, Shayne went on pleasantly, "I don't see any reason we should stand on ceremony. We'll all have to give statements to the police when they arrive, but I don't think a drink will hurt any of us. I'm Michael Shayne, by the way."

One of the men stepped forward with hand outstretched. He was tall and in his forties, with a deeply lined face and an engagingly diffident smile. He said, "I felt I recognized you when you sprinted past me while I was lying on the floor a few minutes ago. I've seen your pictures in the papers, Mr. Shayne. I'm Mark Ames. Wesley's brother." His handshake was surprisingly warm and strong. "If I had reacted more effectively, my brother would still be alive," he said ruefully. "But I was bowled over, you might say, and I was that, literally, when that young man burst into the room waving a pistol in his hand and with murder in his eye. I tried to stop him, but. . . ." He shrugged expressively. "I wasn't very good at football even in college."

"I'm completely in the dark about all this," the pudgy, round-faced man standing behind Mark Ames declared unhappily. The strong odor of whiskey came from him and his eyes were bloodshot behind rimless glasses which were settled firmly on his bulbous nose. "I was upstairs resting in my room waiting for Alfred to bring me a drink when I heard all this commotion downstairs and then in the hallway. A shocking affair. Disgraceful," he told Shayne firmly. "Citizens shot down in cold blood in the privacy of their own homes. A commonplace in Miami, no doubt. Certainly it would not be countenanced in a civilized community. I am told you are a detective, Mr. Shayne. Who *is* that vicious young murderer across the room?"

Shayne said gravely, "His name is Ralph Larson. What's yours, by the way?"

"This is Mr. Sutter, Shayne," interposed Mark Ames quickly. "An attorney from New York City. He flew down this afternoon to consult Wesley on some legal matter and I'm afraid he's gotten a poor idea of our mores here in Miami."

"There have been murders committed in New York, I believe," Shayne commented drily. He turned away as Alfred got to his feet with his burden of broken glass and scurried toward the rear, presumably in the direction of the kitchen.

The outer door opened and Patrolman Powers stepped inside. He looked around the living room and at the five men in some surprise to see them there, and announced loudly, "The Homicide Squad is on the way. Everyone is to stay put until they get here."

"You stay down there, Powers, and keep an eye on them and see that they don't get their heads together and make up any stories," came Griffin's voice booming down from the head of the stairs. "I'm standing guard at the scene of the crime to see that nothing is touched . . . the way it says in Regulations."

Powers called back loudly, "Yes, sir. I'll see to it." He stood with his back against the door and his thumbs hooked inside his pistol-belt, and looked them over sternly. "Just take it easy the way Officer Griffin says," he advised them. "That way, everything will go smooth and we won't have any trouble."

Shayne grinned at him and then crossed the wide room to the settee where Timothy Rourke was seated beside Larson. The younger man sat bolt upright and defiant. He asked bitterly, "What's all this silly rigmarole about? I killed Ames, goddamnit. He deserved killing and I'm glad he's dead. So why in hell don't they put the handcuffs on me and take me off to jail?"

"There's a certain protocol to be followed," Shayne told him. "Take it easy. You'll end up in jail all right. In the meantime, relax. This is probably the last drink you'll have for a good long time," he added as Alfred reentered the room stiffly carrying his silver tray with a pitcher of ice cubes and a carafe of water and an assortment of unbroken glasses on it, in addition to the two bottles of liquor which Alfred had retrieved unharmed from the floor.

Shayne beckoned to the houseman, and asked over his shoulder, "Scotch or bourbon, Ralph? And how do you like it?"

The young man shuddered and shook his head. "I couldn't touch a drop. I think I'd vomit." He hesitated with his young face working queerly. "I keep seeing him *sitting* there grinning at me," he burst out. "I *wanted* to kill him. I *enjoyed* pulling the trigger. But now. . . ." He shook his head dazedly and buried his face in his hands.

Michael Shayne took two cubes of ice from Alfred's proffered pitcher and dropped one of them in each of two tall glasses. He lavishly poured bourbon in one glass and Scotch in the other, added a dollop of water to each and took one glass in each hand, waving Alfred on to the others. He handed the bourbon highball to Rourke who continued to sit beside Larson, and muttered obliquely, "Don't take it so hard, Tim. You did your best, damn it."

"None of that whispering," said Powers sternly from his military stance in front of the door. "I guess it's all right for all of you to have drinks, but there's to be no private communications between suspects until you've each made your statements."

Shayne shrugged and turned away from the two reporters with a glass of watered Scotch in his hand. On the other side of the room Mark Ames had refused a drink, but the New York attorney was eagerly pouring Scotch with a shaking hand into a tall glass containing two ice cubes. He filled it nearly to the top and set the bottle back on Alfred's tray, and lifted the glass to his mouth with both hands gripping it tightly.

Shayne grimly watched him lower the contents by a good two inches before he took it away from his mouth, and he wondered whether Lawyer Sutter was going to still be sober enough to make a statement when Homicide arrived. Not that it mattered much, he told himself. Nothing that Sutter had to tell them could possibly change anything.

Then he heard the low, discreet whine of a carefully controlled siren from the distance on Biscayne Boulevard and knew they hadn't much longer to wait before the efficient technicians from Will Gentry's Homicide Squad took over.

6

SERGEANT GRIGGS WAS A SHORT SQUARELY-BUILT MAN in plain clothes, but his driver who entered the doorway behind him was in uniform. Griggs had an intelligent, weathered face, shrewdly cold eyes, and a completely bald head. He pivoted slowly, just inside the room, scrutinizing each man carefully, and not a flicker of surprise showed on his impassive features as his gaze slid over the detective and the reporter.

With no indication of pleasure, he said, "Well, well. Miami's gift to television and the demon reporter of the daily press. Just what goes on here?"

"There's been a shooting, Sarge. Upstairs," said Powers eagerly. "These fellows claim that one sitting down there did it."

Griggs' gaze rested briefly on the seated Ralph Larson, and then shifted back to Shayne. "Who's the stiff?"

"Wesley Ames," Shayne told him.

"They tell me your secretary called in the first alarm. What do you do . . . get printed announcements when a murder's about to be committed?"

"Not quite. This time it just happens. . . ."

"Skip it for now. Let's go upstairs and get the picture straight. You may as well tag along, Rourke, so we can get full newspaper coverage. That way, you can write the facts for once without having recourse to your imagination. You stay here with Powers," he directed his driver. "Send the other boys on up as soon as they get here."

He went toward the stairs and Shayne and Rourke followed him with their glasses in their hands.

Griffin was standing importantly at attention outside the open door of the study. He said, "Not much work for you on this one, Sarge. Here's the murder weapon." He held out Larson's .38. "I took it off that big redhead while it was still hot and smoking."

Griggs nodded and walked into the room past him, disregarding the gun. "You hang onto it, Griff. Maybe you'll get a citation for discovering important evidence." He stopped and surveyed the sagging door with its DO NOT DISTURB sign still hanging from the knob, then turned his attention to the inner door jamb where a heavy brass socket for a bolt still dangled from one half-withdrawn screw.

"Looks like we not only got murder, but a breaking and entering rap to boot," he observed sourly.

"I'm guilty, Sergeant," Shayne admitted cheerfully. "It seemed like a good idea with shooting going on inside."

Griggs shrugged and walked on into the room, coming to a halt beside the dead man behind the desk and looking down at him fixedly. "He looks dead enough," he observed without emotion.

Wesley Ames did look very dead. In life he had had sharp features, and in death they were tight and pinched. He wore a white shirt without a tie and unbuttoned at the throat, and a heavy, fancy waistcoat of garish red that was tightly buttoned up the front with a row of large silver buttons. The center button was missing. In its place was a round hole where the .38 bullet had entered his body. Around the hole was a wide stain of darker red. Slumped sideways out of the chair as he was, the white leather-cushioned back of the arm-chair showed another round hole where the bullet had come out of the body and entered the chair. Griggs said, "Right through the heart, it looks like. He probably died instantly."

Shayne said, "He was like that when Tim and I busted in not more than sixty seconds after the shot was fired, and he wasn't moving a muscle. I guess he didn't know what hit him."

Griggs straightened up and looked around the room alertly. "This the only entrance?"

"I don't know anything about the set-up and I haven't asked any questions. I'm just an innocent bystander on this one, Sergeant." Shayne looked around the room with Griggs. "That door in the back must open out onto a balcony."

There was a door at the rear of the room on the left that had a wooden bottom and the top half of glass. To the right of the door there were two wide windows, evenly spaced, and both of them were tightly closed and latched on the inside.

Griggs and Shayne walked over to the door together while Rourke watched and listened alertly and made an occasional note. The door had a heavy brass bolt on the inside similar to the one that was fitted to the other door. The bolt was securely pushed inside the hasp. There was an outside light turned on over the door, and peering through the glass they could see a narrow balcony with a wrought iron railing, and a stone stairway leading down to the ground at the side of the house. It was pseudo-Moorish architecture, such as had been much the vogue in Miami in the early twenties.

Sergeant Griggs turned back and investigated the locked windows and muttered, "Everything locked up tight as a drum, with a don't disturb sign on his door." He went back and glanced at the flat top of the big desk. Wesley Ames had evidently been a very orderly man. There was no ashtray, no evidence that he had smoked. A chromium electric coffee percolator stood on a round, heat-resistant pad near the right side of the desk. It had an electric cord plugged into the base that dropped off the side of the desk and was plugged into an extension cord leading to a wall socket. It was the automatic type with a built-in thermostat that shuts it off when it has finished percolating and keeps the contents just below boiling for as long as it is left connected.

Beside the pot was a coffee cup in a saucer, and it contained a slight residue of very black coffee. At the left of the arm-chair in which Ames had been sitting were two wire mail baskets. The one on the left held a dozen or more unopened letters addressed to Wesley Ames. Between the two baskets was a stack of neatly arranged empty envelopes, each one carefully slit open the long way, and the other basket held a pile of letters which had evidently been removed from the empty envelopes.

Directly in front of the dead man was a very modern and very expensive Dictaphone with a gleaming chromium microphone set upright in a holder placed close to the edge of the desk so it could take dictation easily from a person seated behind the desk.

Nothing was out of place and nothing was disarranged in the smallest degree. It gave the impression that the dead man was methodical and orderly, who believed in a place for everything and everything in its place.

Their silent survey of the death scene was interrupted by Griffin announcing loudly from the hall, "Here come your smart laboratory boys now, Sergeant. Not much for them to do this time, I guess.

You want me to hold 'em outside here 'til you're through?"

Sergeant Griggs said, "I'm through in here." He went to the door with Rourke and Shayne behind him and met the technicians of his squad coming down the hall. There was a cameraman with his tripod, the fingerprint expert with his kit, a man carrying a powerful portable vacuum cleaner, with an assistant M. E. bringing up the rear. Griggs waved them into the room saying pleasantly, "Give it a fast once-over, boys. Pictures and prints for the record. And you tell us when and how he died, eh, Doc? Watch it, because this time we've got a pretty good check on your guesswork."

He waited until they passed him into the room and then went toward the head of the stairway, saying over his shoulder to Shayne and Rourke, "Come on with me and let's get some statements on this thing. Then we can all go home and to bed . . . or wherever you two bachelors are going to bed these days."

Downstairs, Ralph Larson was still seated on the settee where they had left him, bent forward with elbows resting on his knees and face buried in his hands.

The attorney from New York was slumped back comfortably in an overstuffed chair with a fat cigar clenched between his teeth and the remnants of what Shayne suspected was his second drink in his hand, and the brother of the murdered man sat bolt upright in a straight chair near the door, nervously smoking a cigarette in a long holder and darting worried glances around the room while he obviously waited for something to happen which he also obviously hoped wouldn't happen.

Sergeant Griggs stopped at the foot of the stairs

and said bluntly, "I don't know who's who around here. Can anyone suggest a private room I can use to talk to some of you people?"

Mark Ames came to his feet lithely. He said, "I'm Wesley Ames' brother, Sergeant. This is Mr. Sutter from New York, an overnight guest. Both Mrs. Ames and Wesley's secretary are out somewhere. The secretary, Victor Conroy, has an office fitted up over here through these double doors in what used to be the library. Is that what you want?"

"Do you live here with your brother?" asked Griggs.

"Certainly not." Mark Ames looked appalled at the idea. "He hated my guts . . . and I his," he went on frankly. "Tonight is the first time I've darkened his doors for months."

"All right," snapped Griggs. "I'll get to you in a minute, Mr. Ames."

He strode toward the double doors indicated by Mark, calling over his shoulder to his uniformed chauffeur who stood by the front door with Powers, "Come in, Jimmy, with your notebook. I'll want some shorthand."

He opened one of the doors leading off the living room and reached inside to switch on an overhead light. Then he turned back and said gruffly, "You first, I guess, Mike. And you come in, too, Tim. We'll get this over as fast as we can."

Two walls of the library were still lined from floor to ceiling with shelves of books, the third wall had a row of businesslike filing cases against it. There was a long refectory table along one side that was littered with newspapers and typed manuscripts and manila folders and with half a dozen leather-seated chairs lined up against the wall behind it, and there was a large typewriter desk in the opposite corner with an electric typewriter and a Dictaphone playback machine on a stand beside it. Griggs chose the only comfortable chair in the room, upholstered in green leather, and motioned the patrolman toward the desk. There were two straight chairs on either side of Griggs, and Shayne and Rourke sat in those.

"Now then," said Griggs. "Michael Shayne being interviewed, Jimmy. Tell us what you're doing here and what you know about this, Mike. Just the simple facts."

Shayne started with Rourke's appeal to him on Larson's behalf that afternoon, said he'd gone out to see Dorothy Larson and got her agreement to break off her affair with Ames, and mentioned dinner at Lucio's.

"We got to my place a little before eight. Tim and Lucy Hamilton and I. The phone rang and it was Dorothy Larson saying her husband had a gun and was on his way to kill Wesley Ames. I hung up and told Lucy to call the cops, and Tim and I came out as fast as we could. Not more than ten minutes, I guess, but Larson's car was already parked in front behind that black Cadillac. We saw the front door open and him run in . . . or somebody run in . . . just as we pulled up. The door slammed shut and there was a shout from inside and then a sort of crash. We ran in and saw Mark Ames lying on his back on the floor and a silver tray with broken glass near the stairs. A man wearing a white coat was just disappearing up the stairs shouting something in Spanish. We ran up, and Alfred . . . in the white coat . . . was pounding on that locked door with the Do Not Disturb sign on it.

"I jerked him back to take a crack at the door, but before I could hit it a gun was fired inside. I had to use my shoulder twice before that bolt gave. Ralph Larson was standing there with a smoking revolver in his hand. Wesley Ames was behind the desk as you saw him. Dead. At least he looked pretty dead to me. I took Ralph's gun, but before I could check Ames your cops got here and Griffin took over. We all got out and Mr. Sutter was outside in the hall with the others . . . Mark Ames and Alfred. He said he'd been in his room when he heard the commotion. We all came downstairs and Alfred cleaned up the broken glass from his tray and brought us fresh drinks. That's about it."

Griggs glanced at Jimmy and got a nod from him. He said to Shayne, "Then it's your testimony that Ralph Larson ran inside this house just ahead of you, knocked Mark Ames down and broke Alfred's tray, ran upstairs and into Ames' room where he bolted the door and shot him to death?"

Shayne said, "I assume that's what happened. I wasn't here and I haven't stuck my nose into your case by asking any questions. All I know for certain is that Ralph Larson was inside that locked room with a smoking gun when I broke in. And that Ames was dead and Ralph *said* he'd killed him."

"He admitted it, eh?"

"He boasted of it."

Griggs turned to Rourke. "Anything to add to Mike's story?"

"I can't think of anything. That's the way it was. But goddamn it, Sergeant, for the record I'd like to say that Ames deserved killing if any man ever did. He drove Ralph to it, and the kid was insane with jealousy. You heard him yourself, Mike. He said that Ames just sat there in his chair and laughed in his face when he said he was going to kill him. He was out of his mind when he did it. If there ever was a case of justifiable homicide. . . ."

"All right, Rourke," Griggs said impatiently. "We're not trying the case here. Wait until you get in the witness chair. You two stick around until I see if any more questions come up. Send the brother in, huh? Mark Ames."

Shayne got up hesitantly, "Do me a favor, Sergeant?"

"I don't know, Mike. Will it cost me my arm?"

Shayne grinned, "Just let me sit back in one of those chairs behind the table out of the way and hear what these other people have to say."

"What the hell for? It's cut and dried, isn't it? All we need to do is get the sequence of things straight."

"I don't know," Shayne said slowly. "I guess I feel more or less responsible for that guy sitting out in the other room with the electric chair in front of him. If I'd paid more attention to Tim this afternoon this mightn't have happened."

"But you did pay attention to me, Mike. You went out and talked to Dorothy Larson as I asked."

"But it wasn't good enough," Shayne reminded him grimly. "I should have talked to Ralph, too. Thrown him in jail, maybe. It sticks in my craw," he went on explosively. "Our getting here just about one minute too late. If I'd got a little more speed out of that car of mine on the Boulevard. . . ."

"If you'd gotten any more speed we'd probably both be dead along with Wesley Ames," Rourke interrupted him.

"Anyhow let's say I don't like to walk out on something before it's finished." Shayne moved around the long table to an unobtrusive seat in the far corner.

Griggs said impatiently, "It's okay by me." He

grinned at Rourke. "Probably just wants a lesson in how a real honest-to-God cop operates. So he can pass it on to his pal Brett Halliday next time he wants to write up one of his cases. That guy could use some lessons in police procedure all right. Ask Mark Ames to come in, Tim."

"Sure." Timothy Rourke was studying Shayne speculatively with very bright eyes. He nodded abruptly and said, "I'll stick around and take a lesson, too, Sarge." He went to the library door and called, "Ames." Then came back and quietly seated himself at the other end of the long table from Shayne.

7

MARK AMES CAME IN AND SEATED HIMSELF QUIETLY in the chair nearest the door. The sergeant said, "This is pretty informal and probably won't even require a sworn statement. We'll see about that later. Mark Ames, Jimmy. The dead man's brother. Just tell me what you know about this, Ames."

"Not much. I was sitting there in the living room waiting for Alfred to bring me a drink when a car came up the drive fast and the floodlights came on outside. They're rigged up that way, with an electric eye at the gate that automatically turns them on when a car turns in. There's also an electric signal system all around the place on top of the wall. Wes wasn't taking any chances on uninvited visitors slipping into the premises."

"Just a minute. Let's go back for a touch of background. You say you don't live here?"

"God, no," Ames shuddered. "I also said, if you recall, that I hated my brother's guts, and you can put that in the record, too."

"Yeh," said Griggs unemotionally. "And you had come here tonight for the first time in months. Why?"

"To talk to Wesley."

"What time was that?"

"After their dinner. About seven o'clock. I had an appointment with Wes and he knew I was coming, but he had that damned don't disturb sign outside his study door and so I had to sit and cool my heels until he was ready to see me."

"Is that your Cadillac outside?"

"Christ, no. I came in a taxi. I think it was a Yellow but I don't know the driver's name or number. You can probably get a record of the time if you want," he added sarcastically.

"All right. Who was here when you arrived?"

"Helena was here. Ames' wife. And Vic Conroy. They and Alfred, the houseboy, live here. I also met Mr. Sutter briefly. He was also waiting to have an interview with my dear brother, having flown down from New York for the privilege, and he was burned up with waiting. He'd also had a few drinks before dinner, I gathered, because he went up to his room soon after I got here saying he was going to rest until the great man would condescend to see him."

"And so you waited in the living room?"

"I waited in the living room. Vic came in here to do some typing, and Helena was nervous and ill-at-ease. She apologized for her husband's keeping me waiting, and Alfred came in soon after with a coffee-pot ready to be taken up to Wes, and Helena took it up. She's the only one in the household allowed in that room when Wes has his sign out. She stayed upstairs and I sat here alone.

"About seven-fifteen the floodlights came on indicating a visitor had arrived, and Vic came out of his room to go to the front door and check him in. It was evidently someone Wes expected, because Vic sent him on around the side of the house to go up the outside stairs to Wes's study.

"That was standard operating procedure here," he went on with a twisted grin. "Wes had a lot of weird characters visiting him at odd hours, and it was Vic's job to know them and screen them, and send them around the back way if they were expected.

"Vic came back inside and talked for a few minutes, and then went upstairs to his own room. A few minutes later Wes's visitor left and the floodlights went off outside. I thought surely Wes would open up his door then and call me to come in, but the son-of-a-bitch didn't.

"Helena came down after a little, wearing a mink and a scarf over her head, and said she was bored to death sitting around this morgue and was going to drive over to the beach for a drink. She said I could tell Wes she'd probably be at the Penguin Club if he gave a damn.

"She was just going out to get in her T-Bird that was parked in front of Wes's Cad when Vic came hurrying downstairs and said he was going in town, too. I remember she asked him if he had Wes's permission to leave the house and he said to hell with that . . . that there weren't any more visitors due tonight and he had some time off due him.

"They went out together and drove off in their own cars." Mark Ames paused, looking at Griggs quizzically. "That brings me up to where I was when I started. Wait a minute. Except that Sutter came to the head of the stairs and yelled down to Alfred to bring him a bottle of Scotch and a glass, adding that he might as well get good and drunk if Ames was going to keep him waiting all night. He was good and sore and I got the impression he was shouting outside Wes's door expecting him to hear him and come out to apologize, but he didn't know my dear brother very well. He went back to his room, and I told Alfred he might as well bring me some bourbon at the same time, and *that* was when the car drove up outside and the lights came on.

"I started for the front door just as Alfred was coming in from his pantry with the tray, and it was flung open violently and a young man burst in flourishing a revolver and shouting, 'Where is he? I'm going to kill him.'

"I tried to stop him, but I didn't try very hard. I didn't like the looks of that gun and I was hardly prepared to give my own life to save Wes. Anyhow, he shoved me aside and ran toward the stairs, and Alfred got in his way and he knocked him aside and the tray crashed on the floor. Then he went up the stairs two at a time, and Alfred picked himself up and went after him, and then the door burst open again and these two men came in. I was just getting up from the floor and all I could do was point up the stairs, and they ran past me and a moment later I heard a shot."

Mark Ames paused and shrugged. "I pulled myself together and went upstairs hoping for the best. Sutter was running down the hall and Alfred was outside the door, and Shayne and Rourke and the young man were inside, and I heard them say Wesley was dead, and I remember my first thought was that a lot of fairly decent people were going to sleep more soundly tonight after hearing the midnight newscast."

Griggs nodded absently. "Is that all, Mr. Ames?"

"Your cops came a moment later. That's all."

"Very well. But stick around until I get through and give you permission to leave."

"I intend to stay at least until Helena gets back. This will be quite a shock to her."

Griggs said, "Send that lawyer in, please," and he lifted his eyebrows at Shayne, "You make any startling deductions from all that?"

Shayne shook his red head. "Nothing startling or otherwise. Brother Mark doesn't make any effort to hide his aversion for the dead man."

"It's pretty much an open secret around town. In fact there are rumors that, well . . . that Mr. and Mrs. Ames weren't entirely lovey-dovey at home and that Mark wasn't averse to filling in while Wesley was tomcatting around elsewhere," offered Rourke.

"You mean he was having an affair with his brother's wife?"

"Just rumors. Helena Ames is a young and lovely woman and Wesley wasn't exactly the ever-loving husband type."

Mr. Sutter came in weaving a trifle and with a half-smoked cigar clenched between his teeth. He said aggressively, "I have no information of the slightest consequence to aid you in this matter, Sergeant. I understand that this man is a newspaper reporter." He jerked his head toward Rourke. "And I find it quite unusual for him to be present at an inquiry of this sort. Highly irregular. My firm will not be pleased if we receive newspaper notoriety in connection with this disgraceful affair."

Sergeant Griggs nodded impassively. "Sit down, Mr. Sutter. State your name, occupation and home address for the record."

He sat down and said icily, "Alonzo J. Sutter. I am an attorney with my office and residence in New York City."

"Is Wesley Ames one of your clients?"

"Certainly not," snapped Sutter, giving the impression that the very suggestion was odious. "I flew to Miami today to have a conference with him on a legal matter concerning one of our valued clients."

"Do you mind giving me his name and stating the nature of the legal matter?"

"I certainly do. That is privileged information and completely immaterial."

"What time did you reach Miami?"

"About five o'clock. I took a taxi direct from the airport with every expectation of conferring with Mr. Ames immediately and I had hoped to return to New York by a later flight tonight. Instead I was greeted on my arrival by the man's secretary, a Mr. Conroy, I believe, who explained that his employer might not be available to me for several hours and suggested that I remain in the house as a guest until such time as Mr. Ames should deign to give me an interview."

"And that made you sore?" suggested Griggs.

"I was naturally indignant, and I protested, but to no avail. I was assigned a guest-room across the hall from Conroy's quarters, and there I cooled my heels until Ames was shot to death."

"Did you have any discussion with him during dinner?"

"He didn't come to dinner. Confound it, the man made no appearance whatsoever. I was served dinner with Mrs. Ames and the secretary, and given to understand that Ames never joined them at the evening meal. That he didn't arise until four or five in the afternoon and secluded himself in his study with only coffee until he went out later in the evening to spend the rest of the night in night-clubs gathering gossip items for his notorious newspaper column. Soon after dinner I went up to my room and tried to nap with the understanding that Conroy would call me the moment Ames was available."

"Did you sleep?"

"Not really. I was naturally quite irritated by the cavalier manner in which I was being treated, and anxious to get the conference over with. After about an hour I came out of my room to the head of the stairs, noting that the confounded Do Not Disturb sign still hung outside Ames' study, and I called down for the houseboy to bring a bottle of Scotch to my room."

"Loudly enough for Ames to hear you inside his closed study?"

"He should have heard me if he wasn't deaf. I intended him to be reminded of my presence and my purpose in his house, but he calmly disregarded that and I went back to my room and shut the door again.

"It was a short time later . . . perhaps five or six minutes . . . when I heard a commotion downstairs and people running about, and I came out of my room to see this private detective and the houseboy outside his door. Then there was a shot from inside, and this man broke the door down with his shoulder. Thus my trip becomes a complete waste of time, and I am informed by the airport that there are no further New York flights available until tomorrow morning. I would like to call a taxi now and go to a hotel in the hope of getting a few hours rest. I certainly don't wish to spend the night under this roof."

Griggs nodded. "In just a few minutes . . . after I clear the rest of this up. Why don't you relax and have another drink?" He turned his head toward Powers who appeared in the doorway, and the young patrolman reported, "Your men say they're through upstairs, Sergeant. And there's an ambulance and stretcher here."

Griggs got up and followed Sutter out, and they heard him conferring briefly in the living room with his technicians, and there were heavy footsteps up and down the stairs, sounds of the outer doors opening and closing, car doors slamming and motors starting.

Griggs returned in a few minutes followed by the houseman who held himself stiffly and self-consciously in the presence of the police. He sat primly erect in the straight chair with knees together and brown hands folded tightly in his lap, and answered Griggs' questions in excellent English.

His name was Alfredo Sanchez, he said, he had been born in New York and held his present position for five years. He was thirty-four years old, unmarried, and claimed he had no police record at all. The household consisted of himself and a colored housekeeper-cook who slept out, Mr. and Mrs. Ames and Mr. Conroy.

He confirmed Wesley Ames' habit of staying out practically all night and generally sleeping until late in the afternoon, and that the columnist seldom took a meal at home. Today he had arisen about four-thirty, Alfred said, and gone directly to his study after he had bathed and dressed, and hung the sign on his door which was supposed to exclude everyone except Mrs. Ames. The cook had prepared a pot of coffee about five, and Mrs. Ames had taken it in to him with a cup and saucer. So far as Alfred knew, no one else had entered the study from the hallway until Ralph Larson had forced his way up the stairs and bolted the door. It was normally never locked on the inside, Alfred explained, because the Do Not Disturb sign was sufficient to insure privacy.

Other visitors who came in the evening were always checked at the front door by Conroy and sent around to the outside entrance where Ames admitted them himself, and he believed there had been at least one such visitor tonight, but he did not know his identity nor whether there had been others or not.

He briefly confirmed the time of Sutter's arrival from the airport, serving dinner to the three of them, Mark Ames' arrival after dinner, and Sutter's retirement to his room some time around seven o'clock.

He had cleared the table and helped cook with the dishes, he said, and she had gone out the back way about seven-thirty as was her custom. He knew that Mrs. Ames and Mr. Conroy had left the house together a little before eight o'clock, though neither had spoken to him or mentioned their plans for the evening.

He had been in his pantry when Sutter called down for a bottle from the top of the stairs, and Mark Ames was alone in the living room still waiting to see his brother when he asked Alfred to also bring him a bottle of bourbon.

He was just emerging from the pantry with the silver tray containing two bottles and four glasses, two of them containing ice cubes, when the front door was flung open and Ralph Larson ran inside brandishing a revolver. He had brushed Mark Ames aside, and Alfred got in front of him as he made for the stairs. He had knocked Alfred and the tray down and run up the stairs, and Alfred followed as fast as he could, but too late to prevent him from entering the study and slamming the door in Alfred's face. Shayne had arrived at that moment, and the rest of it was known to them.

Sergeant Griggs thanked him when he finished his concise recital, and asked him to send Ralph Larson in.

Patrolman Powers escorted the young reporter to the door. Ralph Larson stalked in defiantly and glared at Griggs. "Why can't we get this over with?" he demanded witheringly. "I told you I killed him. Isn't that enough?"

"You haven't told me anything yet," Sergeant Griggs pointed out coldly. "State your name and occupation for the record."

"Oh, for Christ's sake. I'm Ralph Larson. I work on the *News* with Tim Rourke. I shot and killed Wesley Ames upstairs in his study half an hour ago. Is that what you want?"

"There's the question of motive and premeditation," Griggs told him, still coldly. "I understand that you threatened to kill him last night."

"What does that matter now? I was having some drinks with Tim and I shot my mouth off. I'm sure Tim has told you all about it with embellishments." His mouth twisted and he shot a baleful glance across the room at the other reporter. "What the hell does my motive have to do with it? Do we have to drag my wife's name through the mud? I killed him because he was a louse and didn't deserve to live. Isn't that enough?"

"Where did you get the murder gun?"

"It's mine. I've got a permit for it."

"And you came here tonight and burst into the house with a loaded gun, and you planned to kill him?" Griggs said inexorably. "It wasn't a crime of impulse . . . a spur-of-the-moment thing. You've been planning it all day. Is that what we're to understand?"

"I don't give a damn what you understand. I've told you. . . ."

"Don't be a complete goddamned idiot, Ralph," Rourke swore at him. "It wasn't quite as cold-blooded as that. Something triggered you off. Was it something Dorothy said?"

"Dorothy? No. It was that bastard Ames. Sitting there in his chair and laughing in my face when I told him to stay away from Dorothy. I told him I'd kill him and he kept on laughing. So I got my gun and did it, goddamnit."

"Wait a minute." Griggs looked puzzled. "*When* did he laugh at you?"

"This evening. Sitting there at his desk wearing that silly red vest with a row of silver buttons down the front. He didn't even stop opening his mail long enough to listen to me. Sitting there slitting open the envelopes meticulously as though I was dirt under his damned feet. If I'd had a gun then I would have shot him."

"This *evening*? You mean you were here earlier and threatened him and then went home to get your gun and came *back* to kill him?"

"Of course. When do you think I'm talking about? Didn't they tell you I was here earlier? I had an appointment with him, and I didn't bring a gun with me, damn it, so you can't prove I was planning it all day. I was determined to have it out with him, and all I asked him was to promise to leave Dorothy alone in the future. That's when he laughed at me and I decided to kill him."

Sergeant Griggs said, "I think we'd better go back and sort of start over, Mr. Larson. Now then: You had an appointment with Wesley Ames this evening? What time, and what was it about?"

"I was supposed to be here at seven-fifteen to discuss an assignment for tonight. I work ... have been working ... for him on the side. Checking out stories from him about celebrities and getting facts for him to use in his column. I left the office a little early, a few minutes before seven, and drove out here. Vic Conroy came to the front door as usual when I drove up, saw who it was and waved me around to the side of the house where an outside staircase leads up to Ames' study. I rang the bell at the top and he came to the door and looked through the glass, and unbolted it to let me in. He always keeps that door bolted," Ralph went on. He seemed eager to talk now, to make them understand exactly what had happened. "I know that, and that's the reason I didn't go around that way later when I came back. I knew he wouldn't let me in after I'd threatened to kill him, so I came in the front way instead.

"Anyhow, it was about seven-fifteen and he was in his study alone opening his mail and reading it ... or at least glancing at each letter as he took it out of the envelope. I had it all planned ... what I was going to say ... and I started right in as soon as he sat back down at his desk. I told him I knew he was seeing Dorothy at night when he sent me out on assignments, and I asked him ... man-to-man ... to leave her alone. I reminded him that she was young and impressionable, and that he had lots of other women to play around with, and told him he was wrecking our marriage.

"And he sat there in his chair slitting open his goddamned letters and he laughed at me. He said if Dorothy wanted to pass it around he didn't see why he shouldn't get in line for it.

"I would have killed him then and there if I'd had a gun. I told him so. And he laughed in my face. So I went back out and down to my car and drove straight home and got my gun and came back. I hardly remember driving either way or anything." Ralph Larson looked distraught and rubbed a hand vaguely across his forehead.

"Dorothy was there," he said in a perplexed voice.

"I remember she tried to stop me from getting my gun. She tried to tell me that Wesley Ames meant nothing to her and that I had no reason to be jealous of him. But I was halfway out of my mind, I guess. It's all sort of blank until I was here suddenly and running up the stairs and that Puerto Rican tried to stop me. Even then I might not have done it. I don't know," Larson said in a troubled voice. "If he'd just begged me not to. If he'd just paid attention to me and promised, even then, that he wouldn't see Dorothy again. But he was so goddamned superior. He just sat there leaning back in his chair looking at me and not saying a word even when I waved the gun in his face. So I shot him. What else could you do with a man like that? He slid sideways half out of his chair when the bullet hit him, and he still didn't say anything. So, now then!" Ralph Larson lifted his head defiantly and glared at Griggs. "Does that spell everything out for you? I wish I'd had the guts to use another bullet on myself, but I didn't." He dropped his face into his hands suddenly and began weeping.

Sergeant Griggs stood up, looking tired and not particularly happy. He shrugged as Rourke went across the room to stand beside Ralph's chair and put his hand on his shoulder, and walked out of the room and Shayne followed him.

He hesitated outside the door and told the detective, "I guess that ties it up in a neat bundle. You think Tim will be willing to go out with us and break it to Larson's wife? She must be in a hell of a shape, not knowing what's happened to her husband."

Shayne said, "I'll drive Tim to the Larson apartment. It's on Northeast Sixty-First. Are you coming too?"

"Hell, I may as well get her statement for the record, and close it out," Griggs said. "You and Tim go ahead if you like. Get the hysterics over with before I get there."

8

AS MICHAEL SHAYNE DROVE OUT OF THE FLOODLIGHTED area down to the open gate, Timothy Rourke settled back on the seat beside him and sighed feelingly. "Poor punk," he muttered. "What'll become of him, Mike?"

"Ralph Larson? Chances are good he'll burn. You've got premeditation. Actually a killing in cold blood. It's Murder One right on the nose."

"What about the unwritten law?" demanded Rourke. "A man has a right to defend his home ... his wife. This is Florida, after all. Temporary insanity, damn it."

"If he'd done it on the spur of the moment, sure. If he'd just walked in there and shot Ames tonight as we first thought, having worked himself into a state of homicidal jealousy, a jury would probably take a lenient view. If he'd had a gun in his pocket and blasted Ames on his first trip at seven o'clock ... okay. But he left that house determined to get a gun and kill Ames according to his own statement. Half an hour is a long time for temporary insanity to prevail. No, Tim. Any way you look at it your young friend is in a very bad spot. You and I are both to blame for not taking his threat more seriously and stepping in faster."

"Yeh," muttered Rourke. "I'd rather cut off my right arm than break the news to Dorothy. No matter how it looks, I tell you she was really in love with Ralph. Think what she must have gone through this last hour. Ralph dashing out with a gun. She not hearing a word... not knowing *what's* happened."

"There may have been a flash on TV," Shayne suggested. "One of the boys at headquarters may have picked it up." He slid past the traffic light at 79th and eased over into the outer lane to prepare for the turn onto 61st.

"In that case we'll find her hysterical."

"Or under sedation," Shayne suggested hopefully. There were fewer cars parked along the quiet street at this hour than when the detective had stopped by earlier, and he had no difficulty finding a parking place directly in front of the apartment building. He got out with Rourke and they went up the walk together and through the empty entrance hall to the stairway. The doors of both apartments at the top of the stairs were closed and there was silence in the upper hall. Shayne turned to 3-B on the right and pressed the button as he had done on his first visit, but this time he didn't bother to get a pleasant smile ready to greet the occupant when she opened the door.

As before, there was no response to his ring. Shayne hesitated and glanced aside at Rourke with ragged red eyebrows raised questioningly, and pressed the bell again. Involuntarily he caught himself glancing over his shoulder at 4-B, half-expecting that door to open and reveal May Graham, still bare-footed and still welcoming.

But both doors remained shut and only silence answered his second ring. He hunched down and studied the keyhole and jingled a ring of keys in his pocket, and absently tried the knob as he straightened up.

It turned and the door to the Larson apartment swung open. There were lights inside but only silence greeted the opening of the door. Shayne stepped over the threshold, calling, "Mrs. Larson?" and he hesitated only a moment at the entrance to the empty living room before striding in.

The interior arrangement of the apartment was a replica of the one across the hall, with a closed door directly in front of him which he knew opened into a bedroom, and an open door on the right through which he could see a small, neat kitchen.

He heard Rourke enter behind him, and the reporter muttered uneasily, "What the hell do you suppose . . . ?"

Shayne crossed the sitting room in four long, fast strides and jerked open the bedroom door. The overhead light was on in this room also and neatly made twin beds stood side by side, but there were articles of feminine clothing tossed in disarray on one of the beds, a half-packed suitcase stood open near the head of it, and bureau drawers were pulled open haphazardly with contents rumpled and dangling over the edges of the drawers.

Shayne took in the scene with one swift glance, then strode to the open door of a bathroom on the right and switched on the light. Rourke saw him straighten and his shoulders stiffen as he looked inside the bathroom.

Fearful of what he might see inside the bathroom, the reporter edged up behind the rangy detective and peered past his shoulder.

There was no body in the bathroom, as he had instinctively feared. But there was blood on the washbasin and on the floor. And a damp handtowel was wadded up on the floor, liberally smeared with blood.

Shayne turned slowly, shaking his head and looking at Rourke with a deep frown of puzzlement. "I don't get it, Tim. What the hell do you suppose happened here? When she phoned me . . . it was after Ralph had run out with his gun . . . so she said." He paused, thinking deeply. "And Ralph verified that, didn't he? He said Dorothy was here when he came home, and she tried to stop him. Isn't that the way it was?"

"That's what he said. That she tried to tell him there was nothing between Wesley Ames and her. But he also claimed he had pulled sort of a blank and doesn't remember much until he was suddenly at the Ames' house. Do you suppose they actually had a fight and he slugged Dorothy, and . . . ?"

"And did away with her somehow?" Shayne shrugged and turned back into the bedroom, tugging at his ear lobe in deep perplexity.

"From the look of things here she had started to pack a bag. Was that before or after Ralph came to get his gun?"

"Pretty messy packing," suggested Rourke. "Like she was in one hell of a hurry to get out of here."

"And that suggests it was *after* Ralph had come and gone. Or, maybe not. After I talked with her maybe she thought it over and decided to pack up and get out before he came home from the office. Then, if he came back from his interview with Ames and caught her packing a bag, he might have suspected the worst and gone berserk. But that won't work either," he interjected. "There's that telephone call to me *after* Ralph had got his gun and gone back. She must have started packing after she called me. If Ralph then turned around and came back unexpectedly. . . ."

"I don't think there was time for all that," objected Rourke. "It must be a fair fifteen-minute drive from here to Ames' house. Ralph says he first got there about seven-fifteen, had the argument with Ames, drove back to get his gun . . . and then got back there to kill him about eight o'clock. That doesn't leave much leeway for him to have spent here."

"Not if that timetable checks out," agreed Shayne. "Right at this moment we have only Ralph's word for any of it. We don't *know* he had only half an hour to get here and back to Ames'."

"But we do know," argued Rourke, "that not very damned much time elapsed between her phone call and Ralph's arrival there. You didn't waste any time getting there, and he made it just about a minute ahead of us. Even if he drove as fast as you did . . . which I doubt . . . there wouldn't have been more than a few minutes for him to come back and do anything here."

"That's true. Let's get out of here and wait for Griggs without touching anything." Shayne led the way out of the bedroom. "Unless it was some other woman who phoned me pretending to be Dorothy Larson," he went on with a scowl. "I can't say I actually recognized her voice after having heard it only once before."

"What other woman?" demanded Rourke.

"How the hell do I know what other women were involved with the Larsons? There's blood in the bathroom and she's missing, damn it. Just at the time when her husband was committing murder on her behalf. It all adds up to a whole lot of question marks. That'll be Griggs now," he added moodily at the sound of heavy footsteps on the stairway. "He's going to love this . . . just when he had his murder tied up in a neat bundle and was ready to go home and get some sleep."

Sergeant Griggs definitely did not care for what he found in the Larson apartment. He looked at what there was to see, and he listened to what the two men told him, and he wearily went down to his car to have his driver radio in to headquarters for the technical crew to be sent back out to go over the place, and he roughly brought Ralph Larson back upstairs with him without telling him why his trip to jail was being interrupted by a visit to his home, and he shoved the young man inside the living room and he stood in the doorway and watched him and demanded, "Look all around and tell us if this is the way this place was when you ran out with your gun to kill Ames?"

"I don't know what you're talking about." Ralph stood in the center of the neat room looking about dazedly. "Where's Dottie? What . . . where *is* she?" His voice rose shrilly in sudden panic.

"Suppose you tell us."

"But I don't know. I. . . ." He turned and went to the bedroom door and peered inside at the disarray there, shaking his head in dismay. "Dottie was always so neat," he faltered. "She wouldn't have. . . ." He turned to Griggs with his face working. "Where *is* she? What's happened to Dottie?"

"Take a look in the bathroom," said Griggs grimly, stalking up to him with out-thrust jaw. "Then you might try telling us the truth about what happened here tonight. Go on and look." He turned the hesitant young man about and shoved him angrily toward the open bathroom door.

Ralph Larson shambled past the bed and the bureau with its gaping drawers, and looked inside the bathroom. He turned back, his young face white and drawn, his fists clenched tightly by his side.

"Blood all over. Is it Dot's blood? *What's going on here?*"

"Did you kill her first?" demanded Griggs savagely. "And then go back to kill her lover? Where's her body? What did you do with her?"

"I didn't do it. I loved her. That's why I killed Ames. She was here when I went out. She tried to stop me and I remember pushing her. But I didn't *hurt* her. I wouldn't hurt her. I loved her. Don't you understand that?"

"Yeh," said Griggs disgustedly. "You loved her so much you couldn't stand the thought of her getting into bed with another man. Come on! Tell us the truth. What have you got to lose? You've already got one murder rap around your neck. They can only put you in the chair once. Get it out of your system. It'll do you good. You made a clean job of it and killed them both because she was two-timing you."

"I didn't," Ralph cried thinly. "I don't know what you're talking about. Why don't you *do* something, damn you? Don't just stand there. Get busy and find Dottie."

Sergeant Griggs shrugged and turned back from the bedroom door to Shayne and Rourke who were silent onlookers. "This is the kind *I* have to get," he complained morosely. "You, Mike. Can you swear it was the Larson woman who called to send you out to Ames' house?"

"There's no way I can swear to it. She was hysterical and practically screaming at me over the phone. She seemed to know me and about the talk I had with Mrs. Larson this evening. She called him 'Ralph' and she wailed that she didn't want him arrested when I told her she should call the cops. She certainly sounded like a distraught wife trying to head her husband off from committing a murder."

Sergeant Griggs nodded absently. "She probably just got scared and took a run-out powder," he muttered unconvincingly.

Timothy Rourke grinned at him. "After cutting her wrists and bleeding all over the bathroom?"

"How do you know she cut her wrists? How do we even know that's her blood? Maybe she had a nosebleed. Let's don't jump to conclusions around here. After my boys give the place the onceover we'll know more about what went on here. I guess I don't need you two any more," he went on flatly. "Why don't you beat it? I've got work to do."

"Sure," said Rourke easily. "You get on with your knitting, Sergeant. Mike and I'll go get some shut-eye like you suggested awhile ago. How about it, Mike?"

Shayne nodded and edged toward the open door into the hallway. He saw, now, that the opposite door was open about a foot, and he sensed that May was standing behind the partly opened door listening. He stepped out and waited for Rourke to follow him, with his hand on the knob to close the door behind the reporter and with the thought that it might be worthwhile talking to May without interference from the sergeant.

But evidently May had been watching as well as listening, and waiting for him to appear, because her door swung open before Rourke reached the hall, and she swayed forward drunkenly almost into Shayne's arms so he had to catch her to keep her from falling headlong.

She was still barefooted, but she had changed from her former costume into a tightly-belted, pink, quilted robe with a frayed hem that struck her sturdy legs just below the knees. She was quite drunk and her well-fleshed body was heavily lax in his arms as he held her upright. Her eyes were round and unfocussed and she was smiling vaguely and she clung to him and said, "Hiya, Red, honey?" and hiccoughed loudly, and then she drew herself back with dignity and pushed him away from her, and demanded in a huskily fuzzy voice, "Whatcha doin' in there, huh? I thought you was comin' back to see me, Red. Wha' she got that I haven't got, huh?" She stood with arms akimbo and ducked her head coyly and rolled her unfocussed eyes at him.

Rourke stood aside watching with a grin on his lean face, and Sergeant Griggs thrust his square jaw out the door and demanded of Shayne, "Friend of yours, Mike? You didn't tell me. . . ."

Shayne said grimly, "May and I are old friends and I didn't know I was under any obligation to reveal such intimate details to you, Sergeant."

He put his arm gently about May and patted her shoulder beneath the quilted robe. "Where is Dottie?" he asked her quietly. "Have you seen her since I was here?"

She blinked her eyes a couple of times and then closed them tightly and leaned against him. "Haven' seen her," she said in a faraway voice. "Been waitin' for you, Red. Beltin' down a few an' waitin' for you." She snuggled up against him and slowly clasped her arms about his neck, keeping her eyes closed and turning her face up to his with full lips avidly parted. "Send 'em away, huh?" she murmured drowsily. "You take me in an' put me to bed, huh, Red? Tuck me in good?" She pulled his head down with surprising strength, and pushed her mouth up against his, and Sergeant Griggs snorted obscenely behind them and closed the door firmly to shut out the maudlin scene.

Shayne lifted his head from her lips and grinned past her at Rourke and said gruffly, "Help me get her inside, Tim. She's out on her feet and she's a pretty good hunk of woman."

Rourke came up on the side of her and helped support her sagging weight, and they half-dragged her inside and through the comfortably littered sitting room to the still unmade double bed beyond, where they got her decently stretched out and she immediately rolled over on her side and buried her face in the pillow and began snoring gently.

They went out together and closed the outer door behind them just in time to witness the arrival of Griggs' Homicide experts for the second time that evening.

They went past them down the stairs to Shayne's car, and got in and he said, "I'll drive you around to the office, Tim. Got time for a drink first?"

Rourke looked at his watch and grunted his satisfaction. "Time for half a dozen. I want to check with Griggs again and maybe have another talk with Ralph before I write my story."

9

MICHAEL SHAYNE STOPPED IN FRONT OF A SMALL BAR around the corner from the newspaper office where he often met Rourke for a drink, and they went inside together, past a line of men at the bar and with a greeting for the bartender, and back to an unoccupied booth near the rear.

A waiter came also immediately with drinks which the bartender had automatically started making as soon as they walked in, a tall, very brownish bourbon and water for the reporter, and a brimming shot-glass of cognac for Shayne with a tall glass of ice water on the side.

Shayne nodded and said absently to the waiter, "Keep them coming, pal. As fast as we get low." He took a cigarette out of a crumpled pack from his shirt pocket, lit it reflectively and let twin spirals of thin gray smoke trail from his nostrils. "What do you make of it, Tim?"

"I don't." The gangling reporter took a long slow drink, lowering the contents of his glass halfway. "I don't get that picture in the apartment at all, Mike. Where could Dorothy Larson be? Suppose she did take out after Ralph after phoning you, with some crazy idea of trying to stop him?"

"After spilling blood all over the bathroom?"

"It could be nosebleed. We still don't even know it's her blood. A neighbor kid might have cut his finger and she bandaged it for him."

"That's right." Shayne took a long sip of cognac and chased it down with a swallow of ice water. "We do know she never got to Ames' house if she started there." He paused, rubbing his chin thoughtfully. "They don't have a second car, do they?"

"No. That is . . . no, they don't. I remember Ralph mentioning that recently. It's one of the reasons he needed the extra money he was earning from Ames."

"What did he actually do for Ames? I don't know much about the man except that his gossip column was widely syndicated and he was regarded as Miami's Walter Winchell."

"What did Ralph do?" Rourke shrugged. "Sort of legman, I guess. Went around to night spots and gathered items for Ames' column, or checked on rumors of gossip that are the stock-in-trade of a scavenger like Ames. I wouldn't be surprised if he had a couple of others on his payroll doing the same sort of thing. God knows he earned enough from his column to afford as much help as he needed."

"How much?" Shayne asked with interest.

"How much did he pay?"

"How much do you suppose his column earned him?"

Timothy Rourke emptied his highball glass while he considered the question. Shayne drank from his glass again, and the waiter reappeared with refills for each. "Hard to say," Rourke admitted finally. "I never had a syndicated column but I do know something about prices. At a rough guess: Thirty to fifty thousand a year. Maybe more."

"Then he wasn't what you'd call hard up?"

"Not exactly. That would be gross, of course, but he didn't have much overhead. Whatever pittances he handed out to boys like Ralph. And his secretary, of course. He was full-time, I understand."

"I was thinking," Shayne said, "about a couple of remarks made by Mark Ames. One was to the effect that a lot of people were going to sleep more soundly tonight after they heard that Ames was dead. Would he be implying that his brother, who he quite evidently detested, was not above a spot of blackmail?"

"Not necessarily blackmail. Wesley Ames was certainly feared and hated by a lot of people. He couldn't help picking up stray bits of very damaging information about many celebrities during his night club rounds which might even ruin a career if printed in his column. In other words, he was certainly in a good position to do some discreet extorting, but I never heard him charged with that. I think he enjoyed the power it gave him over many important people, and it probably gave him sadistic pleasure to watch them writhe while they waited for his columns to appear and see what he printed about them."

"So a lot of people will sleep easier tonight after they hear the good news," muttered Shayne.

"Not much doubt about that. What does this have to do with Dorothy Larson's disappearance?"

"Damned if I know." Shayne sipped his cognac morosely. "It's just that the whole thing is thrown wide open by what we found at the Larson apartment. It may be pure coincidence, of course, and have nothing whatever to do with Ames' death. But if she doesn't turn up pretty soon with a logical explanation of where she's been, we'll have to assume otherwise and start looking in the cracks for things that aren't apparent on the surface. If Ralph, for instance, was trying some private blackmail on the side . . . and Ames got wind of it . . . ? Don't you see? Maybe it wasn't just a cut-and-dried case of sexual jealousy after all, and Ralph had some other impelling motive that no one knows about . . . except maybe his wife. Hell, I don't know," he went on disgustedly. "At this point it's just a matter of pure theorizing. Maybe Dorothy Larson just went home to mama for the night. Does she have a mama in town?"

"I don't know. I suppose Griggs will check out all the relatives and close friends with Ralph."

"Yeh. Griggs is a careful and thorough cop." Shayne emptied his cognac glass and scowled down into it. "There's something bugging me," he muttered. "Something about that locked room murder set-up that smells just slightly. But it smells, Tim. I can't put my finger on it. It was there for me from the very beginning . . . even when I accepted all the surface indications. With Dorothy Larson inexplicably missing, and that bloody bathroom staring us in the face, I'm getting a stronger and stronger hunch that everything isn't exactly as it seems." He shrugged his wide shoulders and angrily tugged at his left ear lobe.

Timothy Rourke sat very erect and peered across the table at him with bright, alert attention. During the years that he had followed Michael Shayne around on his cases he had learned to have a profound respect for the redhead's hunches. "What is it?" he urged. "What is it that smells, Mike?"

"I wish I knew. There's something that keeps eating at the back of my mind. Something in Ames' study that was out of place. Or something should have been there that wasn't." He shrugged and looked up at the waiter who was approaching the booth inquiringly, and shook his red head firmly. "No more for me." He got out his wallet and gave the man a bill, and Timothy Rourke finished his drink and sighed and said reluctantly, "I'd better get into the office myself and see what's on tap. Are you calling it a night?"

Shayne said, "Lucy will be sitting on the edge of her chair and chewing her fingernails waiting to hear what happened after we dashed off."

But after they parted outside the bar and Rourke swung around the corner to the newspaper, Shayne sat in the front seat of his car for at least sixty seconds before turning on the ignition.

And then he didn't drive to his hotel to satisfy his secretary's curiosity. Instead, he stopped in front of the Miami Police Headquarters and parked in a space that was plainly marked "Reserved For Official Cars Only." He went in a side entrance and down a hall to the left and climbed one flight of stairs and entered an open door into a small office that held a littered desk with Sergeant Griggs sitting behind it. The sergeant was studying a sheaf of reports and he glanced up with a thoroughly unwelcoming frown at the redhead who pulled up the only other chair in the office and sat down. He grunted sourly, "I thought you were bedded down for the night. That barefoot gal in the apartment across from Larson's looked drunk enough not to mind *who* she slept with."

Shayne shook his head and said cheerfully, "You're a liar, Sarge. You know damned well you went into her apartment to try and question her about the Larsons, and you found her quietly passed out in her own bed all by her own sweet self. What did your boys turn up after I left?"

"Nothing," growled Griggs wearily. "Not one damned thing that's any good to us. No fingerprints of any significance. Nothing. Best we can make out of it . . . she started frenziedly packing a suitcase as though she were in a hell of a hurry and got interrupted or changed her mind for some reason. No one in the building saw her leave. No one, goddamn it, saw Ralph Larson come back this evening to get his gun and go out to kill Wesley Ames. Nobody saw nothing," he ended disgustedly.

"What about relatives or close friends she might have gone to?"

"Larson says they haven't got either one in town. The guy's either a hell of an actor or he's just about off his nut with worry about her. He appears to be a hundred times more concerned about her than he is about a little thing like murder," Griggs went on bitterly. "It just hasn't got through to him that he faces the chair for killing Ames. The young fool is proud of it."

"You got the M.E.'s report on Ames?" Shayne asked abruptly.

"Yeh. It's here some place along with the typed statements from the witnesses." Griggs shuffled listlessly through the papers in front of him. "There's nothing in it. What the hell do you expect? Wesley Ames is dead. Shot through the heart with a steel-jacketed thirty-eight that came out through his back and embedded in the chair. Ballistics says it was fired from the gun Larson handed you when you busted in. Death was instantaneous and occurred between half an hour and an hour before the body was examined. No unusual fingerprints in the room. Nothing. What the hell should there be? Everything was tied up in an absolutely perfect neat knot with premeditation and every other damned thing tied tight around Ralph Larson's neck and not a single unanswered question about the case until his damned wife turns up missing with blood all over the place."

"Her blood?" asked Shayne interestedly.

"How the hell do I know?" snarled Griggs. "When we find her we'll take a sample and find out. Just like a woman to complicate an open-and-shut case. First she incites her husband to commit murder, and then she disappears and throws a monkey-wrench into the proceedings."

"Yeh," said Shayne sympathetically. "Women are like that. Jezebels, that's what they are. I don't see why men put up with them. It would be a simpler world without them."

"Simpler, maybe, but I don't know, Mike. Where'd the kids come from?"

"There is that," Shayne agreed. He switched back abruptly to business. "Did you say you have the typed statements of the witnesses there?"

"Yes. Not that there's anything in them you haven't already heard."

Shayne said, "Could I see Sutter's statement? I want to check one point."

"Sutter? That lawyer from New York. It's here." Griggs fumbled through the papers, extracted two typed sheets stapled together and slid them across the desk to the detective.

Shayne took it and glanced down the first page swiftly, turned to the second page and stopped near the end to read the final paragraph carefully.

He handed it back, narrowing his eyes and rubbing his blunt chin thoughtfully. He nodded his head slowly, his eyes bleak and questioning, while Griggs watched him, puzzled but interested.

They had never been closely associated on a case before, and Griggs had the professional policeman's innate distrust for private detectives and their methods of operation, but he was fully aware of Shayne's long record of brilliant successes in the solution of cases, many of which had been bungled by his own police department, and he was not one to pass up any help no matter where it came from.

He asked gruffly, "You find anything there that I missed?"

Shayne said, "I don't know. I'm beginning to get an inkling of something that's been bothering me. Let's see Ralph Larson's statement."

Silently, Griggs sorted it out from the others and passed it over.

Again, Shayne glanced swiftly down the typed lines to a point near the end where he paused and read the confessed killer's words carefully. He put it down in front of him and looked across at Griggs and said flatly, "I think we both missed something. Where is Ames' body now?"

"In the morgue for the time being. Pending funeral arrangements."

Shayne leaned forward and said, "If you're a smart cop you'll order a P. M. on him, Sergeant."

"A post mortem? What the hell for? We know exactly when and how he died."

"Do we?"

"Are you completely nuts? You were there. You're one of the main witnesses."

Shayne leaned back in his chair and half-closed his eyes.

"We know that Ralph Larson shot him through the heart with a thirty-eight calibre bullet about sixty seconds before I broke the door down. Your medical examiner says the bullet passed through his heart and that the wound would have caused instant death. How much time elapsed between the firing of the shot and the medical examination?"

"You were there through it all," growled Griggs. "Say twenty minutes. Thirty at the outside. You were the one who said he was dead by the time you broke the door down and got inside."

Shayne said evenly, "Check my statement if you like, but I think this is what I said: 'That he looked pretty dead to me. But before I could check him, the radio cops got there and Griffin took over.'" He stopped to think a moment and added, "The way it was, Griffin was so busy holding a gun on me that he had Powers check to see if Ames was dead. Powers is nothing but a rookie, Griggs. If we reconstruct everything carefully, we'll discover that Powers is the only person who touched Ames or even went close to him during all that time until the M. E. got there. I'm sure Powers is a smart lad, but I don't believe he's had much experience with dead bodies. No one else can testify with certainty concerning Ames' condition."

"Do you mean to say, goddamn it!" exploded Griggs, "that you're suggesting the bullet *didn't* kill Ames?"

Shayne nodded emphatically. "That's why I want a P. M."

"But damn it to hell," fumed Griggs. "A thirty-eight slug through his heart! You've got the M. E.'s report. What more do you want?"

"Thirty minutes after the shooting," Shayne reminded him. "After a completely superficial examination. There was no reason for it to be more than that," he went on swiftly and placatingly. "All of us knew . . . or thought we knew . . . exactly how and when Ames died. The M. E. had no reason to question the evidence and make anything more than the most superficial examination. But now I think a post mortem is definitely called for."

"I'd be the laughing-stock of the department."

"Maybe. Also you might prove to be one of the

smartest homicide dicks south of the Mason-Dixon line. Look," Shayne went on persuasively. "Discounting the curious disappearance of Dorothy Larson and the half-packed bag on her bed and the bloodstains in her bathroom . . . which you have to admit give an aura of mystery to the whole affair . . . discounting that, take a look at these statements of Sutter and Larson."

Shayne handed the two typewritten statements back to him. "Read the end of Sutter's statement first. The last line of the next to final paragraph. It says: '. . . I went back to my room and shut the door again.'

"Then, first line of final paragraph: '. . . I heard a commotion downstairs and people running about. . . .' That is Sutter's statement, isn't it?"

Griggs read the words, frowning. He nodded without looking up.

"He was at the end of the hall with his door shut," Shayne pointed out. "He heard Ralph force his way in downstairs and up to Ames' study. Isn't it reasonable to assume that Ames would also have heard the same commotion?"

"Probably. No one says Ames didn't. He didn't testify on the subject."

"But Ralph Larson did in a sense. Read the end of *his* statement. He's speaking of Ames acting so superior when he ran in waving his gun: '. . . He just sat there leaning back in his chair looking at me and not saying a word even when I waved the gun in his face . . .' What does that suggest to you?" demanded Shayne.

"A pretty cold-nerved customer. Remember, he had already sat and laughed at Ralph half an hour earlier when he threatened him."

"That's what I am remembering," Shayne said

grimly. "It's one thing to sit and laugh in the face of an unarmed man, and another thing to sit there in a chair and calmly invite a bullet in your heart without even making a move to prevent it.

"Think about this a minute. Ralph Larson has stormed out the back way from the study half an hour previously threatening to get a gun and kill Ames. Ames isn't frightened by the threats and he sits right there. Okay. Half an hour later he hears a commotion downstairs . . . the same one Sutter heard. Ralph shouting, the tray breaking, feet pounding up the stairs to his study. What does he do?

"*Nothing,* by God. He doesn't even get up from his chair. He sits there . . . silent and grinning . . . and gets a bullet in his heart. What does that suggest to you?"

"That he was drugged or something?" hazarded Griggs.

"There was that pot of coffee on his desk," Shayne reminded him. "No one thought about analyzing it, of course. A post mortem will show it up fast enough if it was drugged. I'm just saying there appear to be some unanswered questions, Sergeant, and I think you'd be smart if you get the answers to them before this case ever comes to trial and the defense attorney starts asking for proof that his client's bullet actually killed the man."

"Yeh," Griggs said slowly. "You've sold me a bill of goods, Shayne. It sure as hell can't hurt anything . . . and with Mrs. Larson being missing and all. . . ."

He nodded his bald head decisively and got up from behind the desk. "If anything comes out of it you'll get the credit," he added generously.

Shayne said, "Forget the credit, Sergeant. I just

want one favor. Let me know the minute you get the P. M. report. No matter what time of night."

"You'll get it," promised Griggs, and he hurried out of his office with Shayne following at a slower pace behind him.

10

MICHAEL SHAYNE AGAIN PARKED HIS CAR AT THE CURB in front of the side entrance to his hotel because he expected Lucy Hamilton to be waiting for him upstairs and that he would drive her home a little later.

He climbed the one flight of stairs that by-passed the elevator and went down the hall toward his door, instinctively getting out his key as he approached. He unlocked the door and it opened silently and the ceiling light was still on as he had left it when he dashed out a couple of hours previously.

But Lucy wasn't there to jump up and greet him with eager curiosity as he had expected. He advanced slowly into the room, noting the tray with the glasses still on it where he had set it down on the center table to answer the telephone, with the liquor bottles standing beside it where Rourke had placed them.

He stopped and looked around uncertainly, and then a broad grin spread over his rugged features. Lucy lay curled up asleep on the shabby sofa against the right-hand wall. She had kicked off her shoes onto the floor beside the sofa and she lay on her side with her cheek nestled into the palm of her left hand, and she was breathing as sweetly and quietly and happily as a child that has been bedded down with loving care by its mother after having said its prayers in full confidence that they will be heard.

Shayne moved over slowly and silently to stand at

the head of the sofa looking down at his sleeping secretary, and his grin widened when he saw the book lying open and face down where she had dropped it on the floor. It was a copy of *Michael Shayne's Long Chance*, a mystery novel which Brett Halliday had written from one of his cases, the story of his first meeting with Lucy Hamilton in New Orleans soon after his wife had died, when she had been one of the prime suspects in a murder case and long before either of them dreamed she would eventually wind up as his secretary.

He leaned down to pick the book up to see how far she had read, and was touched to find it was open at page 169, at the point in the story where he had asked her to decide whether she wished to take a long chance with him on a wild hunch which he hoped would blow the case wide open. That was when he had called her 'Lucile' and she had said to him then, "I think I know you better, Michael Shayne, than I've ever known any man," and her eyes had been shining and her voice confident as she said it those many years ago.

He turned away slowly with the book in his hands, and laid it face down on the table beside the tray and poured cognac into the empty glass waiting there.

A long time ago, and a great many things had happened since that day in Lucile Hamilton's New Orleans apartment when she had first thrown in her lot with him. He tipped his head back and let cognac trickle down his throat and wondered if Lucy now regretted that decision she had made in New Orleans. There had been good times and bad times for each of them, and out of it all they had built an enduring relationship which was as close to marriage as either of them wanted.

He lowered the glass and turned his head to look at Lucy again, and he saw her eyes were sleepily half-opened and fixed on him although she had not moved from her sleeping position.

She said drowsily, "I've been dreaming, I guess. I was reading that book, Michael, and I got to thinking back. . . ." Her voice trailed off and she closed her eyes again and a little half-smile of contentment came over her softly flushed features.

Then she opened her eyes wide and pushed herself up on the sofa and fluffed her brown curls with both hands and said practically, "It was that champagne I drank at dinner. You shouldn't have given me so much. You know my capacity."

"Tim Rourke was paying for it," he reminded her.

She blinked her eyes at him, and suddenly frowned and demanded, "What happened, Michael? You and Tim dashed off to try and stop his friend from shooting the columnist. I called the police as you told me, and then I sat here waiting. What happened?"

"We were about a minute too late to head Ralph Larson off," he told her. "Wesley Ames is dead and Ralph is in jail charged with murdering him."

"Oh no!" she cried instinctively. "That's too bad. I don't know them, of course, but it all sounds so useless."

Shayne nodded somberly. "Most murders are. You want a drink now, angel? You were about to have a C and C when I got that call."

Sitting on the edge of the sofa, Lucy shuddered as she leaned down to slip on her shoes. "That was hours ago and the champagne has all worn off now. I'd like a nice tall glass with ice cubes and cognac and filled to the top with soda. Then you can tell me all about Ralph Larson and Wesley Ames. I'll go in the bathroom to comb my hair and put my face back on. I feel *quite* dishevelled and practically wanton."

Shayne chuckled and told her, "You looked like an innocent child asleep there on the sofa." He took the tray into the kitchen to get fresh ice cubes and open a bottle of soda, and the telephone started ringing as he returned with the tray.

Lucy was coming out of the bathroom and Shayne stood by the table with the tray in his big hands scowling down at the instrument. "I'm afraid this isn't our night for quiet drinks, angel. If we're lucky that'll be Dorothy Larson calling again."

"Why lucky?" asked Lucy curiously, and Shayne realized that she didn't know about Dorothy being missing. He set the tray down and picked up the phone, but this time it was the voice of the desk clerk from downstairs:

"There's a man to see you, Mr. Shayne. He says it's very important."

"Who is it?"

"Mr. Sutter, he says. From New York, and he has to see you at once."

Shayne said, "Send him up," and put the instrument down and scowled at Lucy and tugged at his ear lobe. "A lawyer from New York named Sutter," he told her. "He was at the Ames house waiting to see the man when he was killed. I don't know what he wants with me, but he's on his way up." He shrugged his shoulders and poured a generous dollop of cognac into a tall glass holding three ice cubes. He filled the glass to the top from the bottle of Club Soda and handed it to Lucy just as a knock sounded on the door. He told her, "I'll get it," and went across the room to admit the pudgy figure of Alonzo J. Sutter.

Shayne nodded pleasantly to the New York attorney, noting that the man carried himself more erectly than before and that his round eyes behind the rimless glasses were not as bloodshot as they had been. He said, "Come in, Mr. Sutter. Perhaps you'll join us in a drink." He closed the door and turned to wave a big hand at Lucy who was gracefully settling herself in one of the comfortable chairs with her glass in hand. "My secretary, Miss Hamilton," he said formally. "This is Mr. Sutter, Lucy."

Sutter nodded vaguely toward Lucy and said, "I'm delighted," in a tone which belied his words. He shook his head firmly at Shayne and said, "No drinks, please. I came here hoping and expecting to have a very private talk with you about a very confidential matter, Mr. Shayne. It is of vital importance," he went on severely. "I made inquiries about you after you left the Ames residence, and I ascertained that you are highly regarded locally as a discreet and competent private investigator. I wish to consult you in your professional capacity," he ended abruptly, again with a doubtful glance toward Lucy and the array of liquor bottles and glasses on the table.

Shayne laughed easily and put his hand on the rotund attorney's elbow and guided him toward a chair near Lucy's. "We couldn't be any more private," he said cheerfully. "I assure you that Miss Hamilton is the soul of discretion." He pushed Sutter down into the chair and turned to the table, adding, "Let me know if you change your mind about a drink."

He poured himself a noggin of cognac and sat down comfortably in a deep chair across from Sutter and Lucy, and said, "I thought you'd gone to a hotel for the night and were catching an early plane back to New York."

"I am at a hotel. The Costain on Third Avenue. And I have a reservation on a plane departing at nine A.M. for New York. But I am hesitant to leave Miami with things at loose ends as it were. Earlier in the evening, when I first became aware that Mr. Ames had been shot, it appeared to me that in a sense my mission was accomplished . . . that I could rejoice whole-heartedly and return to New York to inform our client that all was well and that . . . er . . . he had nothing further to worry about.

"However, afterthoughts began to worry me. The death of Mr. Ames does not necessarily settle the affair I came here to negotiate. The question now arises: Who will take possession of his private papers? What disposition of his effects will be made? Will his widow, perhaps, or his secretary, continue his syndicated column? Who will control what will be printed in the future?"

"How does that concern you or your client?" Shayne demanded bluntly.

Mr. Sutter sighed and he blinked his eyes rapidly behind the rimless glasses. He settled himself more deeply and comfortably in his chair and reached inside his coat to take a fat cigar from the breast pocket. He bit off the end and got a lighter from a side pocket and put flame to the cigar. He pursed his thick lips and expelled a cloud of smoke, and began speaking as though each word he uttered was distasteful to him:

"I came to Miami on a very definite and unpleasant mission. In my briefcase at the hotel I have an envelope containing twenty-five thousand dollars in currency which I was authorized to hand over to Wesley Ames in exchange for documents in his possession which would be ruinous to one of our valued clients if printed in Ames' newspaper column. I am opposed to extortion and to the payment of blackmail in any form. The very thought is abhorrent to me. But I had no choice in this matter. I came here prepared to act for our client and make the exchange in good faith. Now, Ames is dead. I realize that the documents in question must be there in his study, accessible to whoever goes through his private papers and takes possession of them. I realize now that I will have failed my client if I return to New York tomorrow morning without those papers in my hands. That is why I am here, Mr. Shayne."

"Why?" demanded Shayne.

"It seems to me that you are in a position to recover them at once, before someone else finds them and realizes their possible value. You appear to have the full confidence of the local police and it should not be difficult for you to gain access to the dead man's study tonight on some pretext. The papers must be there at hand. All arrangements were made and Ames expected to turn them over to me tonight."

"Just what are these 'papers' that you were prepared to pay twenty-five grand for? What am I supposed to look for?"

"They consist of certain original documents highly incriminating to our client," Sutter told him primly. "I hesitate to divulge his name, but I must trust you I suppose. He is Alex Murchinson. The name may be unknown to you, but he is high in the councils of our city government and the documents consist of private agreements with certain prominent contractors in the city relating to what might be referred to, vulgarly, as kickbacks or payoffs for the awarding of certain contracts for services to be rendered the city. It was highly irregular and most imprudent for Mr. Murchinson to have such documents in his possession while vacationing here recently," Sutter went on severely, "but some of the details were finalized here where it was convenient and safer to meet some of the other parties concerned without arousing suspicion.

"They were stolen from his hotel suite on the night of his departure for New York," the attorney continued, "by a woman who had insinuated herself into his confidence and was evidently in the employ of Ames for just such nefarious purposes. I have in my pocket photostatic copies of the original documents which were mailed to our client after his return to the city, with the thinly-veiled threat that unpleasant details would be subsequently printed in the Wesley Ames syndicated column unless payment of twenty-five thousand dollars was made to him. It was my intention to compare the photostats with the originals before turning over the money to Ames."

Shayne held out a big hand and said, "Let's see what I'm supposed to search for in Ames' study ... providing I can get in for a look."

Sutter hesitated unhappily. "I ... don't know. I suppose I *can* rely on your discretion. This is a very delicate matter...."

"Yeh," said Shayne grimly and coldly. "I can see just how delicate it is. You've got a crooked city official conniving with crooked contractors to mulct the city out of money by passing out contracts on a kickback basis. If you want me to do anything for you hand over the photostats so I know what I'm looking for. If you don't, get yourself and your stinking proposition out of here."

"Really, Mr. Shayne!" Sutter looked astonished, hurt and shocked by this outburst. "I'm not at all sure...."

"Make up your mind fast," snapped Shayne, getting up and turning to the table to pour himself another drink, and broadly winking at Lucy as he turned. "Normally," he said with his back turned, "I consider a blackmailer a vicious scoundrel who deserves to be stamped on. But some blackmailees deserve any damned thing they get and it sounds to me as though your valued client Mr. Murchinson is in that category. If I had a syndicated column to do it in I'd probably publish the damned documents, and the only thing I really blame the dead man for is making a deal not to publish them. Are you going to give me the photostats or not?" he demanded harshly, turning back with his filled glass in one hand and holding the other out to Sutter.

"I certainly do not care for your attitude, but under the circumstances I fear I have no choice." Sutter withdrew a long white envelope from his pocket and passed it over with what remnants of dignity he could muster.

Shayne sat down and opened the envelope, drew out some folded photostatic copies of legal-sized sheets and glanced through them briefly. He nodded and returned them to the envelope and handed them back to Sutter.

"All right. I'll see what I can do. I don't know whether there will be a police guard over Ames' study or not."

"There is," Sutter told him. "I heard that sergeant directing that a man be stationed there before I left. That is why I thought of you and the possibility that you might be able to gain access to the room even though it has a police guard."

Shayne said, "I might be able to work something." He looked across at Lucy and her glass which was still half-full. "Drink up, angel, and I'll drop you off home on my way up to Ames'."

"Ah . . . about your fee, Mr. Shayne. If you are successful in recovering the evidence. Do you think a thousand dollars . . . ?"

"I think," said Michael Shayne blandly, "that twenty-five grand will be exactly right."

"Twenty-five . . . *thousand?*" wailed Sutter. "For possibly half an hour's work. That's preposterous. I cannot possibly. . . ."

Shayne got up from his chair and towered over the pudgy seated man, his blunt jaw out-thrust.

"You said you had an envelope in your hotel room containing that sum which you brought down here for the specific purpose of buying those papers. If they were worth that much three hours ago, they're still worth that much. Don't talk to me about any thousand bucks. Me, I've got at least as much probity as your client in New York. I'll do your dirty job for the full twenty-five grand, but not a penny less. Take it or leave it."

He turned away angrily and drained his glass and slammed it down on the table.

Mr. Sutter got up behind him and said weakly, "Well I . . . I was authorized to pay that amount, of course. It's still extortion," he went on bitterly, "but. . . ."

"It's legal extortion this time," Shayne told him cheerfully. "I'm simply getting paid for doing a job. Go on back to your hotel and wait for me to call you. If I have any luck it'll be within an hour." He stood by the table and watched Sutter turn and go out of the room.

11

WHEN HE TURNED HIS HEAD THE REDHEAD SAW LUCY looking at him over the rim of her glass with a smile of tolerant exasperation. "You are the damnedest bundle of contradictions, Michael. That poor little man . . . it *is* extortion, you know. Pure and simple."

"You know what that poor little man had in the back of his mind?" Shayne demanded cynically.

"He was just doing his job, Michael. Trying to save his client money."

Shayne said, "I wish I had your faith in human nature, angel. Saving his client's money, hell! If I'm any judge of character he was hoping to go back to New York with the evidence in hand. Mission accomplished. Period. With twenty-four thousand bucks in cash stuck deep into his own pocket while I'm supposed to be grateful for one lousy grand for doing his dirty work for him."

"Does collecting twenty-five thousand for the job instead of one make it any less dirty?" demanded Lucy with spirit.

"No. Not really. But it sure as hell salves my conscience. How else can I afford to buy you mink coats and things?"

"I haven't got a mink coat."

"Just what you need to salve *your* conscience," Shayne told her enthusiastically. "We'll go mink shopping tomorrow *if* I collect from Sutter tonight." He glanced at the empty glass in his hand and then at his watch. "Finish your drink and let's go."

Lucy Hamilton wrinkled her nose at him and finished her drink. They went out together and down the stairs to his car, and as they drove off she reminded him:

"You never did tell me why you thought that call would be from Dorothy Larson and that you'd be lucky if it was. Why lucky? Why did you expect her to call you?"

"I hoped it would be a call about her, at least. We don't know where she is or what's become of her." He swiftly explained the condition of the Larson apartment when he and Rourke went there after the shooting. "What does your woman's intuition make of that . . . in view of all the known circumstances?"

"The last we know about her is when she telephoned you to say her husband had run out of their place with a gun and she was afraid he was going to shoot Wesley Ames? Is that right?"

"That's the last anyone seems to know about her."

"And there's a half-packed suitcase on the bed, her clothes scattered around, and blood in the bathroom," Lucy recapitulated thoughtfully. "I don't *know*, Michael. She would naturally be terribly frightened and distressed. Your earlier visit must have worried her frightfully. I wonder. . . ." She paused. "Under the circumstances do you suppose she might have called Mr. Ames to tell him the way things were going?"

"Do you mean after she talked to me and before Ralph came back? Or after Ralph went out with a gun and she called me . . . to warn Ames?"

"Well, I really meant after you talked to her. While she was sitting there planning what to say to

Ralph when he came home. If she was having some sort of affair with Ames, wouldn't she be likely to call him to break it off?"

"U-m-m," ruminated Shayne. "And maybe he was serious about her. Maybe he said, 'To hell with that husband of yours, babe. Pack a bag and get out of there to avoid a violent scene.' Is that what you're thinking?"

"I hadn't gone that far," Lucy said honestly. "But it might have been that way. And if Ralph came back unexpectedly and caught her packing. . . ."

Shayne slowed and turned off the Boulevard onto Lucy's side street. He said slowly, "I'm trying to remember whether there was a telephone in Ames' study. I'd suspect he'd have a private line there, but I don't recall seeing one. It's where he closed himself up to do his work, and maybe he didn't have one. Normally I suppose his secretary would handle his calls. It's something I'll have to check on if I can get in there tonight."

He drew up at the curb opposite Lucy's apartment, and got out to go across the street with her and wait in the little foyer while she unlocked the outer door of the building. She turned with the door held open and lifted her face to his, and he gave her a gentle goodnight kiss, and she said, "Be careful, Michael. Don't get into any trouble over a measly twenty-five thousand dollars. I honestly don't need a mink coat in Miami."

He grinned and patted her shoulder and promised, "I'll let you know how it turns out . . . if it isn't too late."

He went across to his car whistling under his breath and telling himself he had a mighty fine secretary and one who deserved mink if any secretary in Miami did.

The driveway and parking area in front of the Ames house were dark when he approached the gateway, but lights showed in both the first and second stories of the house.

The floodlights came on automatically and almost blindingly as he turned in between the gateposts, and there were now two cars parked behind the black Cadillac sedan. The police cars and Larson's compact were gone, but there was a cream-colored, open, convertible Thunderbird and behind it a late-model Pontiac.

Shayne pulled up behind the Pontiac and got out in the bright glare of the floodlights, and the front door opened and a man stood there looking at him as he approached.

He was a young man with a slender well-knit body, wearing a yellow polo shirt that was molded to his muscled shoulders and a pair of dark tan slacks. He had close-cropped, burnished black hair and a thin black mustache that was shaved to make a straight line across his upper lip, and he had mobile, intelligent features.

He blocked the doorway so that Shayne stopped directly in front of him, and he said with cool aloofness, "I think you must be Mike Shayne, the private eye. I understand you were here once before tonight. What is it this time?"

Shayne said, "Some unfinished business. Are you Conroy?"

"I am . . . yes. I understood that the police investigation was closed."

"My private investigation isn't," Shayne told the secretary in a tone that matched his. "What's the protocol here? Do you get out of my way or do I push?"

"For heaven's sake, let the man in, Vic," came

Mark Ames' tired voice from the interior of the room. "If he has any further questions let's get them answered and done with."

Victor Conroy shrugged his shoulders with a faint hint of insolence, and stepped backward quietly out of the doorway. Shayne entered and nodded to Mark Ames who stood at the end of a wide brocaded sofa at the right with a highball glass in his hand. A tall, slender, elegantly-gowned woman was slumped back on the sofa beside him with her long legs carelessly crossed to expose a couple of inches of silken-clad thigh, and with a sullen expression on the darkly Semitic beauty of her face. She, too, held a highball glass, and she looked as though she had been belting down drinks in a hurry.

Ames nodded back to Shayne and looked down at the woman, and said, "It's Mike Shayne, Helena. The detective who tried to get here in time to save Wes's life but was about sixty seconds too late."

"Well, thank God for that." The widow straightened her shoulders and her intensely black eyes were luminous. She spoke concisely, with no slurring of her consonants. "Why did you come back, Mr. Shayne? To collect the medal you so richly deserve for getting here sixty seconds too late?"

"Now, Helena," said Ames worriedly, dropping the thin fingers of his right hand to touch her shoulder lightly. "It isn't necessary to be too blatant about the way you feel."

She shrugged and said, "I doubt whether this red-headed man gives a damn one way or the other how I feel. And if he does, he can lump it. Can't you, Mister?"

Shayne nodded impassively. "I certainly can, Mrs. Ames. It's a pleasure to meet a forthright female."

"Hear that, Mark? He's not a snivelling hypocrite.

He must have known my dear departed husband because to know him was to hate him. Did you hate him, Mr. Shayne?"

"I didn't know him that well." Shayne turned away from the murdered man's brother and his widow to the secretary. "I'd like a word with you, Conroy."

Victor Conroy shrugged and said, "Okay by me. We've already told the police all we know."

"Shall we go in your office?" Without waiting for Conroy's acquiescence, Shayne led the way into the room that Griggs had used earlier. He waited by the double doors until Conroy was inside, then closed them saying, "I've got a hunch those two in the living room would just as leave be alone with their grief."

Conroy allowed himself to smile reluctantly at this. "My former boss had a way about him," he admitted wryly. "Helena shouldn't get tanked up like this . . . not while Mark's around. Not that it matters much I guess," he went on sourly. "Ralph Larson did them both a favor by knocking Ames off the way he did. You can't put a woman in jail for admitting she's glad her husband has been murdered."

"How about you?" demanded Shayne. "Are you joining in the general rejoicing?"

Conroy shrugged his shoulders and met the detective's gaze squarely. "I've lost a job. Wesley Ames was a son-of-a-bitch to work for, but he paid well."

"What will become of the column now?"

"It'll automatically be canceled. He was a few weeks ahead and the papers will run those, I suppose. But the column *was* Wesley Ames. No one can step into his shoes."

"What I'm wondering," said Shayne softly, "is

who will inherit his files? The bits of nasty gossip he's collected but has never printed about a lot of important people."

Conroy seemed not to understand what Shayne was driving at. "I suppose it's all part of his estate," he said indifferently. "His widow inherits so far as I know."

"Will she be likely to keep you on the job for a time? To sort things out and catalog them?"

"I doubt it." Victor Conroy scowled darkly. "More likely she'll just consign everything to the incinerator without even looking at the files. She hated his column," he explained. "She hated the sort of man it had turned him into. She liked the money it brought him, but that's all she did like about it."

Shayne lit a cigarette and looked inquiringly about the secretary's office, letting his gaze come to rest on the filing cabinets along the wall. "Did he keep all his material in here? Did you file it all?"

"All that he trusted out of his own sight. He had personal stuff in his desk upstairs that he considered too explosive for even my eyes. He went to a lot of trouble to explain that to me one day," Conroy went on angrily. "He was guarding me against temptation, he told me. There was stuff that couldn't be printed because it would ruin people's lives if it were, and he was afraid I might use it for blackmail if I got my hands on it." Conroy shrugged. "To hell with it. He's dead now and I won't say I'm sorry."

"So far," said Shayne flatly, "I haven't found anyone who is. Did he have a telephone in his study?"

"No. It was one of his idiosyncracies. That was the Master's Sanctum Sanctorum. When he closed that outer door and hung the Do Not Disturb sign out he was alone with his conscience. Which means he was pretty damned well alone," Conroy interpolated with a contemptuous smile. "Anyhow, he wouldn't stand for any interruption except for special visitors who had definite appointments and whom I was supposed to send around to the outside stairway where he would unbolt the door to let them in and bolt it when they left."

"Like Ralph Larson this evening?"

"Yes. Ralph had a seven-fifteen appointment and he arrived promptly."

"Did you take any telephone calls for Ames this evening?"

Conroy hesitated, thinking back. "No," he finally said decisively.

"Did Ames have any other appointments except the one with Larson?"

Conroy said, "No," without hesitation.

Shayne thought a moment and said, "That's about it, I guess. I'm going up to check one thing in the study, and then I guess you people will be left alone."

He turned to open the door into the living room and Conroy told him, "There's a policeman on guard outside the study with orders not to admit anyone. God knows why. The murder is all solved, isn't it? They've got their killer."

"It's just a police regulation," Shayne told him vaguely. "According to the rule-book, you seal off the scene of death for a certain period to make sure no clues are disturbed."

He went out and crossed the living room toward the stairway, noting out of the corner of his eye that Mark Ames and Helena were seated very close together on the sofa and the widow appeared to be getting all the comforting she needed.

At the top of the stairs he saw Patrolman Powers

comfortably settled in a chair opposite the sagging door into the study, with a small table beside him that held a coffee cup and saucer and an ashtray. The young patrolman had his nose buried in a paperback, but he looked up alertly when Shayne reached the top of the stairs, and put down his book and got up slowly, saying uncertainly, "Hello, Mr. Shayne. You're back, huh?"

Shayne said, "Griggs was tied up at headquarters and he asked me to stop by and check one point for him in the study." He casually started past Powers inside the room, but the uniformed youngster said earnestly, "Wait a minute. No one is supposed to enter that room. Those are my orders."

Shayne paused in front of the door and turned with a grin. "Griggs didn't tell you to keep me out, did he?"

"Well, no. Not specifically you, no, sir. But on the other hand. . . ."

Shayne sighed. "I know how it is. An order is an order. You haven't been on the Force very long have you, Powers?"

"No, sir. Only three months since I finished probation. But I. . . ."

Shayne nodded indulgently. "You'd better run down and call Griggs on the phone and check. He's not going to like it, but . . . look," he said brightly. "Instead of bothering the sergeant and getting him sore at you, why don't you call the chief? Will Gentry. Get him to vouch for me. If he isn't still in his office I'll give you his private telephone number at home. Tell him Mike Shayne wants an official okay to go into the murder room and look for a piece of evidence that Sergeant Griggs asked me to look for."

"Well, hell," said Powers. "I wouldn't want to

bother Chief Gentry, I guess." He knew Shayne's reputation, of course, and that he *was* a close personal friend of the police chief, and he had seen Griggs apparently take the redhead into his confidence that evening, and he decided, "You go ahead. Just don't take anything out without showing me, huh?"

Shayne said, "Certainly *not*," as though that was positively the last thing in the world he would think of doing, and he pushed the unlatched door inward on its sagging hinges and stepped inside and closed it firmly behind him against Power's curious eyes.

The study looked exactly as it had before except the dead body of Wesley Ames had been removed. Shayne went to the desk swiftly and began opening the drawers and examining them expertly. There was printed stationery in one, envelopes and stamps; and two others held thin Manila folders, each marked with a name and carefully arranged in alphabetical order.

Shayne looked for Murchinson at once without finding the name. He checked back carefully to see he had made no mistake, and then opened a couple of the folders at random and glanced at the material they held. There were penciled jottings and notations, dates and names which were meaningless to Shayne, but there were three photographic negatives in one of them which Shayne held up to the light and then dropped back into the folder. He replaced them with no doubt in his mind that this was the "explosive" stuff which Conroy had mentioned, raw material for blackmail.

But there was nothing with Alex Murchinson's name on it. Shayne hastily went through all the other drawers in the desk without finding anything interesting, and he straightened up to look around the room for some more secreted hiding place, a wall safe or some such, when the door suddenly swung inward without warning and Sergeant Griggs plowed over the threshold and confronted him angrily.

"All right, Shamus," he growled. "If you've found whatever it is I sent you up here looking for, you can hand it over to me."

12

MICHAEL SHAYNE HESITATED A MOMENT, SEEKING TO gauge the sergeant's temper and to decide how to handle the situation.

He said, "I'm sorry, but I couldn't find it, Sarge."

"*What* couldn't you find?"

It came to Shayne then, in a sudden flash of intuition. The thing that had bothered him about the locked death room to make the picture complete.

"His paper-knife," he told Griggs. "Whatever it was that he used for slitting open his envelopes so neatly." He gestured toward the stack of empty envelopes between the two mail baskets on the desk, each one of which had been carefully slit open the long way.

"Do you remember what Ralph Larson said about his earlier visit to Ames? He said something like: '. . . he sat there in his chair slitting open his goddamned letters and he laughed at me.' What was he slitting them open with? I can't find any letter-opener here, and I've looked in all the drawers. I got to thinking about it and it bothered me so I came out to check my recollection."

There was a curious baffled look of mingled exasperation and pleasure on Griggs' face as he listened to Shayne's bland explanation.

He said, "You're sure about that, huh? No paper-knife."

"Not unless he had a special hiding place for it that I haven't found."

Griggs nodded and turned to call through the open door behind him, "Powers. Get that secretary up here."

Powers said, "Yes, sir," and they heard him going toward the head of the stairs.

"It's a funny thing you thought about that," Griggs said heavily. "What would a missing paper-knife have to do with Larson shooting the guy?"

Shayne replied honestly, "I haven't figured that out either. That's why it didn't impinge in the beginning, I guess. Because it didn't seem to matter. But when I started wondering about Mrs. Larson and thought about Ames just sitting there and making no effort to defend himself when Larson broke in. . . ." He stopped in mid-sentence and shrugged as Victor Conroy came in and said, "You wanted me, Sergeant?"

"Yeh. We're wondering what sort of implement Ames used for opening his mail." Griggs pointed a blunt finger at the stack of empty envelopes. "Those are all cut open."

"Yes. He always used a paper-knife. It should be right there on his desk. It always was." Conroy moved past the sergeant, frowning at the bare top of the desk. "It was a fancy one of brass or copper. Sort of a Florentine dagger thing. An antique, I guess. It had a long thin pointed blade that was honed to razor sharpness on both edges. That's funny." Victor Conroy shook his head and frowned. "It was always right here in plain sight. Maybe one of the drawers?"

Griggs shook his bald head. "We've looked in the drawers. Do you remember the last time you saw it?"

Conroy shrugged and shook his head. "It's not the sort of thing one notices. You know, it's always lying there day after day. It looks as though he used it to open his mail this evening."

Griggs agreed flatly, "Yeh. It does look that way. All right, Conroy. I want to talk to all of you a little later. No one is to leave the house."

The man hesitated as though about to protest the order, but checked himself and went out of the room.

Griggs moved about restively for a moment, clasping his hands behind his back and disregarding Shayne. Suddenly he swung on him and demanded bitterly, "Why don't you ask me what the P. M. turned up?"

Shayne asked obediently, "What did the P. M. turn up?"

"Wesley Ames was dead before the bullet went into his heart. He had been stabbed in the heart with a knife that had a long thin pointed blade sharp as a razor on both edges."

"Something like an antique Florentine dagger," Shayne said interestedly.

"Damn it, you don't act surprised. What sort of prior knowledge did you have? If you've been holding out information on me, Shayne. . . ."

"I haven't been holding out anything," the detective assured him earnestly. "It just all falls into place suddenly. We can even see how we were all mistaken, thinking Larson's bullet killed him. It must have gone through his vest about the same place as the stab wound. It wouldn't bleed a great deal, and the blood would be soaked up inside the vest. No one opened it up to notice that the blood was already congealed until the M. E. got here twenty minutes later, and by that time he couldn't tell without making extensive tests. My God!" he exclaimed suddenly. "Larson didn't commit murder after all. All he did was fire a bullet into the body of a corpse. What irony."

"Shooting with intent to kill," muttered Griggs. "We can hold him on that."

"What a terrific stroke of luck for the real murderer. The wildest sort of coincidence. He couldn't possibly have planned it that way even if he had *known* Larson was coming back here with a gun to kill Ames. It was one chance in a million that Larson would actually fire without realizing Ames was dead, and that the bullet would go in the same wound and destroy evidence of the stabbing."

"Yeh. Whoever did it must be shaking hands with himself right now and figuring he's in the clear with Larson ready-made to take the rap for him."

"One of the four people downstairs," Shayne pointed out to him thoughtfully. "We know he was alive when Larson stormed out the back way. Ames bolted the door behind him. They all say no one else came up the drive and in the back way after Larson. It has to be one of those four, Sergeant."

"Wait a minute. We don't know that Ames was still alive when Larson went out. Suppose he did it then? Picked up the knife and stabbed him."

"And then came back half an hour later to do the job openly with a gun?" scoffed Shayne.

"Well, he might have figured that would give him an alibi for the real killing," argued Griggs stubbornly. "He wouldn't expect his bullet to go in the same hole, and would expect the stab wound to be discovered immediately. By God, that would be smart," Griggs went on, warming up to the idea. "If he did work it like that, he must be sitting in his jail cell right now sweating blood and waiting for us to discover the truth. The poor bastard can't *tell* us to have an autopsy and look for a stab wound. Talk about your ironic situations. By God, Mike," the sergeant went on wonderingly. "It *could* be that way. If it hadn't been for his wife being missing and you getting suspicious and wanting a P. M., he could have gone to the chair for shooting a dead man. And maybe it would be justice because maybe he stabbed him in the first place."

"But Dorothy Larson is missing," Shayne reminded him. "I hardly see how that ties in with your theory. And don't forget that back door bolted on the inside. Ames couldn't have done that with a knife wound in his heart."

"How's this? Maybe Ames didn't bolt the door. Maybe one of the others in the house came in here after Larson left and found him stabbed. So they bolted the door and just walked out the other one without saying anything."

"If one of the people in this house found him dead and the door unbolted, they'd know Larson was the killer. By bolting the door behind him they would immediately take all suspicion off Larson and make each one of them suspects. It's the last thing in the world any of them would do."

"I guess you're right." Griggs looked unhappy and chewed on the knuckle of his left thumb. "That gives us those four . . . counting the houseboy . . . and that New York lawyer, too. The way I remember their statements, any one of the five could have had an opportunity to slip in here between the time Larson left and when he came back. Sutter was up here, supposed to be in his room alone with the door shut. Mrs. Ames was up here doing something unspecified. Conroy came up to his room for a time before deciding to go out. Mark Ames claims he was downstairs all the time, but he was alone in the living room after Mrs. Ames and Conroy went out, and he could have slipped up here. So far as we know, Alfred didn't come upstairs, but I suppose there's a servant stairway up the back, so *he's* not out. Damn it, the thing is wide open, Mike. And I don't know whether you caught any of that by-play between Mark Ames and the widow or not, but neither one of them is doing much grieving. You remember what Tim Rourke said about the two of them, and rumors around town they were having an affair."

Shayne nodded, tugging at his ear lobe. "If I were you, Sergeant, I think I'd *try* to find out why Mark Ames had come out tonight for the first time in months to talk to his brother."

"Yeh, and I also want a line on Mr. Sutter, the attorney from New York, and why *he* was here to see Ames. It didn't matter before when I thought it was a cut-and-dried shooting, but now it does matter. Now I'll have to hold him in town ... Goddamn it, Mike!" Griggs broke out explosively. "Why did you have to get so smart? You and your damned post mortem! I never will get any sleep tonight."

Shayne grinned and said, "You're a cop. You get paid by the city for not sleeping. Me, I don't." He pretended to yawn widely. "It's all yours, Sarge."

"Goddamn it, Mike! You tear this thing wide open with your lousy post mortem ... are you just going to walk away and leave it that way?"

"I'm leaving it in your very efficient hands, Sergeant Griggs. I'm headed for some well-earned shuteye. Hell, you've got it narrowed down to five suspects and about half an hour of time," he said indulgently. "What more do you want in a murder case?"

"Yeh," said Griggs unhappily. "Five suspects that hated the dead man, and not a clean-cut alibi for a single one of them. Okay. Get out of my hair," he said with finality. "Go get your shut-eye or whatever private dicks do on their nights off while honest cops are working for a living. Just don't come back messing up this case with any more of your smart ideas. If you get any more like that, keep 'em to yourself, hear?"

Shayne drew himself to attention and saluted smartly. "Very well, Sergeant. I shall away." He turned and strode stiffly out of the room and down the stairs where Mark Ames and Helena were still huddled together rather intimately on the sofa, and where Victor Conroy intercepted him on his way to the door with a worried look on his face.

"Why is that policeman so interested in Wesley's paperknife, Mr. Shayne? He was shot to death, wasn't he? Suppose the knife is missing? There might be a dozen reasonable explanations for that?"

Shayne shrugged and countered, "You never can tell what sort of crazy tangent a homicide dick will go off on. It's an occupational disease."

"But what did he mean by ordering that no one should leave the house?" demanded Conroy, following Shayne to the door. "Does he have a right to issue orders like that?"

Shayne told him, "A cop in charge of a murder investigation has pretty much blanket authority. I wouldn't argue with Griggs if I were you. He's only doing his job." He went out into the flood-lighted area and down to his car with the sergeant's official car parked closely behind it. The uniformed driver got out from under the wheel as Shayne opened his door, and he hurried forward to ask anxiously, "Do you know if I'm supposed to wait out here, Mr. Shayne, or does the sergeant need me inside?"

Shayne said, "I think he's going to be taking some more statements and will be wanting your shorthand pad. Wish him luck from me," he added with a wide grin, backing up against the front bumper of the police car and cramping his wheels to make a left turn back down the driveway.

When he reached his hotel this time, Shayne put his car into its assigned slot in the hotel garage, and walked around to the front entrance to the lobby.

The desk clerk watched him with interest as he crossed the lobby toward the elevator, and called out, "There's a phone message for you, Mr. Shayne."

Shayne broke his stride to go to the desk, and the clerk got a slip of paper from a cubbyhole and handed it to him. Shayne unfolded it and read: *"Call me at once."* There was a telephone number and a room extension, and it was signed *"Sutter."* Shayne went on to the elevator and up one floor and to his suite where there was still ice water and a bottle of cognac waiting for him on the center table.

He poured a drink and sipped from the glass contemplatively, spreading the telephone message out on the table and scowling at it. It had been received almost an hour previously, very shortly after Sutter had walked out of this room.

He sat down and lit a cigarette and called the number Sutter had given, and when a happy female voice answered, "Hotel Cos*tain*. May I help you?" he gave her the extension, and the attorney's voice came over the wire. "Yes?"

"Mike Shayne. Is that Sutter?"

"Yes. Thank goodness you called, Mr. Shayne. I've been worried. . . ."

"I just got back from the Ames' house," Shayne cut him off. "I told you I'd be in touch as soon as I had anything to report."

"I know you did. What *have* you to report, Mr. Shayne?"

"Nothing good," the detective told him bluntly. "I went through the man's private files without finding anything on your client. Yet, I'm sure I had the real dirt . . . the stuff he had no intention of printing."

"I'm not surprised," Sutter told him. "You see, I received a call in my room immediately after I got back from talking to you. A man who refused to identify himself told me that he had the information in his possession . . . the documents concerning my client which I had come down here to buy. He quoted a paragraph from one of them which convinced me he was telling the truth, Mr. Shayne."

"And?"

"He is willing to turn them over to me for payment of twenty thousand dollars. He is apparently aware that Ames' price was twenty-five, but as an inducement for me to deal with him at once . . . he stressed it must be tonight . . . he will accept twenty . . . intimating that I could pocket the extra five and no one would be the wiser."

Shayne asked, "Why are you calling me?"

"Because I don't trust the man whoever he is. I am not accustomed to dealing with violence, Mr. Shayne. He set up a midnight rendezvous to which I agreed reluctantly. What assurance have I that he will not meet me and forcibly take my payment without delivering the documents?"

Shayne said, "It has been done. How is the pay-off set up?"

"He gave me definite instructions. At midnight exactly I am to walk out the front entrance of my hotel and hail a cab . . . the first one waiting in line at the cab-stand or the first one that cruises by if none is waiting. He warned me that I would be under observation from the moment I stepped out the door and got into the taxi, and that if it were followed by another car the deal would be off. He gave rather elaborate instructions to prevent the possibility of my being followed unknown to him, and I confess I cannot see how you can circumvent them. But I suppose private detectives have a great deal of experience in such matters and I hope you may arrange to be on hand when I turn the money over to him."

Shayne said, "Go on. What were his instructions?"

"To proceed north from my hotel at a moderate speed to Sixty-seventh Street. Left on Sixty-seventh for five blocks, and I am to instruct the driver to slow down in the middle of the fifth block and pull into the curb on the right and stop there for at least a full minute. I am then to tell the driver I have changed my mind about getting out there, and for him to drive on to the next corner where he is to turn south and drive slowly in that direction until we are hailed by a car and directed to pull over and stop. He will be in that car with the documents."

Shayne had been jotting these directions down as the New York attorney gave them to him. Now he said, "I've got all that, Sutter. If you want to take that dope back to Murchinson in New York I advise you to do exactly as he says."

"And you?" asked Sutter anxiously.

"Don't worry about me. This is my town and this sort of thing is my business. Don't look for me out of the cab. Don't expect to see me following you. Remember that if you are able to see me, your man will too. Just have your driver do exactly what he told you to. I'll be in on the payoff, don't worry about that, and you'll be fully protected all the way."

"Very well. I confess I don't see how . . . but that

is your business, isn't it? Shall I take the full sum with me, or only twenty thousand?"

"All of it," Shayne directed him. "In two envelopes will be best. You're going to owe me the five if all goes well and you turn the twenty over to him."

"Yes, I . . . I was afraid you'd drive that sort of bargain," said Sutter sadly. "But I don't care. If I can just conclude this unsavory business successfully and get back to New York I shall be most happy."

"One more thing," Shayne said sharply. "Have you been contacted by Sergeant Griggs?"

"The policeman who came to the Ames house? Not since I came to the hotel. I understand that he had no further interest in me."

"That situation has changed," Shayne told him. "He's going to be looking for you to ask some more questions." He looked at his watch and went on, "If you want to be certain to be free to leave your hotel at midnight, I suggest you get out of your room right away and stay out of it. There's a cocktail lounge downstairs in the Costain. Go down there and settle yourself in a booth with a drink until twelve o'clock, and don't pay any attention if you're paged. Later on, if Griggs does contact you, you needn't tell him I warned you to keep out of his way."

"Of course not, Mr. Shayne. But why on earth . . . ?"

"We'd better not waste time discussing it now. The sooner you get out of your room the better. Griggs is likely to be sending a man around for you at any moment." Shayne hung up and sat back comfortably to finish his drink and to wonder who it was that had the Murchinson papers in his possession, and how he had come by them.

13

AT FIVE MINUTES BEFORE TWELVE A BELLBOY CAME through the cocktail lounge of the Costain Hotel in downtown Miami sing-songing, "Call for Mister Sut-ter. Mister Alonzo Sutter. Call for Mister Sutter."

Seated alone in a shadowed booth near the entrance, Alonzo Sutter turned his head slightly and put his left hand up to instinctively shield his face from the passing boy. He had a feeling that everyone in the bar was looking at him and wondering why he did not answer the summons, though he knew that was utter nonsense because no one in the lounge could possibly know his name was Alonzo Sutter.

It was the second time within half an hour that he had been paged like that, and it gave him a guilty feeling to realize it must be the police who were looking for him. The two envelopes in his pocket containing five thousand and twenty thousand dollars added to his guilt feelings. He wasn't accustomed to carrying large sums in cash, and the fact that the money was earmarked as a blackmail payoff made him feel like a furtive criminal as he sat in front of an untasted drink and waited for the final minutes to pass.

It had been bad enough when he first accepted the assignment in New York, but at that time it had seemed a relatively simple matter to fly to Miami and deliver an envelope to a well-known syndicated columnist, with a return reservation at ten o'clock which he had deemed would give him ample time to conclude the unpleasant affair.

He looked at his watch and sighed, realizing that he would have been in New York right now had things gone according to schedule. But there had been that infuriating delay at the Ames house when he arrived shortly before six. Wesley Ames' secretary had admitted that he was expected to arrive from New York, although he implied he did not know the exact nature of Sutter's business, but the man absolutely refused to disturb his employer's privacy to announce Sutter's arrival.

He would simply have to cool his heels and await the great man's convenience, he was informed, and both Conroy and Mrs. Ames had been vague about the time Ames could be expected to emerge from his study and make himself available. They had been kind enough to give him dinner and offer him a room for the night when it became apparent that he was likely to miss his return flight.

In his irritation, Alonzo Sutter had drunk more cocktails than he was accustomed to before dinner, and had emptied his wine glass several times during the excellent meal.

Then had come the disgraceful shooting affair, with the house filling up with private detectives and reporters and the police, and with Sutter's realization that he had failed to accomplish his mission in Miami.

And now it was one minute and thirty seconds until midnight, and he reluctantly began to slide out of the booth to keep his appointment with a blackmailer who was unknown to him. He had paid for his drink when it was served him, and he left a modest tip beside the still untouched glass. He nervously checked his watch again as he went from the dimness of the cocktail lounge into the well-lighted lobby, and he strolled toward the street door at a pace calculated to bring him out onto the sidewalk precisely at midnight.

There was no doorman on duty at this hour and Sutter walked to the curb and stood there in the bright light of a street lamp and looked to his left toward the taxi-stand. There were no empty cabs waiting, but as he stood there he saw one approaching, and he waved to it and it pulled in and stopped in front of him.

The attorney got into the back seat and closed the door, wondering nervously who was watching him from what vantage point, wondering if Michael Shayne was about, and *where* he was, and how he would manage his part of the assignment.

His driver was slouched behind the wheel wearing a vizored cap tilted down over his eyes and with the butt of a cigar clenched between his teeth. Without turning his head to look at his passenger, he spoke around the cigar in a Southern drawl, "Whereabouts you-all wanta go, Mister?"

"Uh . . . straight ahead driver. Due north to Sixty-seventh Street, and not too fast if you don't mind. On Sixty-seventh I want you to turn west for a few blocks and I'll give you further directions at that time."

The taxi jerked forward away from the curb, and the driver threw back over his shoulder in a surly voice, "Tell me where you wanta go, Mister, an' I'll take you the quickest way. We got through streets in this man's town an' I know how to beat the lights."

"Straight north to Sixty-seventh," repeated Sutter

firmly. "And not too fast, if you please. I'm a little early." He turned to peer out the back window, wondering if the taxi was being followed, but he gave up the attempt after a moment, realizing that it really didn't make any difference whether it was or wasn't.

Actually, he told himself, if he were either the blackmailer or Michael Shayne, he wouldn't bother trailing the taxi away from the hotel. The instructions he had been given specified a one-minute stop on 67th in the fifth block west of 3rd Avenue, and that was where contact could most easily be made. He settled back as comfortably as he could, sniffing the unpleasant aroma from the cheap cigar his driver was smoking, and got a Perfecto from his own pocket and lit it to help quiet his nerves and offset the offensive odor from the front seat.

The taxi moved steadily north at about thirty-five miles an hour. Sutter hoped and believed that pace would fit the "moderate speed" requirement given him over the telephone, and he congratulated himself upon having a driver who was willing to follow a fare's instructions without argument. He shuddered to think what most New York taxi-drivers would do if asked to drive not too fast. He didn't like Miami or anything he had seen of the city, but their taxi drivers, he thought, had a great deal to commend them.

They were well out of the business section of the city now, and into the northern residential district, and the driver mumbled over his shoulder and past the foul-smelling cigar, "Sixty-seventh, you said, Mister? And you want I should turn left there?"

"Left, yes. For a few blocks. I will tell you where to stop. And I appreciate the way you're holding the speed down."

"All the same to me, Mister," said the driver philosophically. "I got all night behind this wheel. If you ain't goin' nowhere special it's a cinch I ain't neither."

He slowed as he approached an intersection, made a left turn and Sutter saw the sign for 67th Street as they passed it slowly.

He leaned forward and carefully counted the blocks. As they slid past the fourth intersection, he said nervously, "Slow down please. It's in this block. On the right-hand side. There. Up beyond those two parked cars. Pull in to the curb, please."

His driver followed his instructions without comment, but as he reached forward to pull up his flag on the meter, Sutter said hastily, "Keep your flag down, driver. I'm not quite sure . . . that is . . . I'd like to wait here in the cab just a minute until I decide whether or not. . . ." He let his voice trail off uncertainly, wondering what reason he could give the driver for pausing here and then driving on as he had been directed, but the man solved that problem for him by chuckling lecherously and ending his sentence for him, ". . . whether or not her husband's home? Is that it, Mister? Lemme know when you make up your mind." He belched comfortably and expelled a thick cloud of noxious smoke toward the rear of the cab.

When the attorney was certain they had been stopped at least sixty seconds, he said, "I think I'll just ask you to go on, driver. Turn left at the next corner, please, and head back toward town. But not too fast, please. I may change my mind after all. I can't quite decide. . . ."

The cab pulled away from the curb slowly and evenly, but the driver's good nature appeared to be lessening as he said in a surly voice, "Games we're playing, huh? Okay by me. I got all night like I said."

Sutter sat tensely looking back as they approached the next corner, and he saw lights switched on in a car that was parked on the opposite side of the street behind them, and it moved out as they made the turn and started southward.

But only one car had picked up the trail there. That would be the blackmailer, he had no doubt. Then where was Shayne? The detective had given his word to be present at the payoff, but Sutter was desperately afraid that Shayne had failed him somehow. He kept his head craned back, watching to the rear, and he saw the headlights of a single car swing around the corner behind them, also going quite slowly, but gradually increasing speed so it cut down the distance between them.

Still there was no sign of the private detective. There was no other car at all moving in either direction on the empty street, and the one behind them was moving up now, and Sutter clenched his Perfecto tightly between his teeth and resigned himself to handling the situation as best he could with no help from Michael Shayne.

The taxi continued to cruise south sedately in the righthand lane, and the following car was coming up fast. It swung out to go around the taxi on the left, and Sutter saw that the driver was a man, alone in the car. As he came abreast of them he honked his horn three times, shortly and sharply, and began to turn in to force the cab to the curb on the deserted street.

His driver exclaimed, "Hey. What the hell?" twisting his wheel to the right to avoid a collision, and Sutter leaned forward and said hastily, "It's all right, driver. A ... friend who wants to talk to me.

Just pull in and stop."

The taxi eased in to the curb and stopped, and the other car did likewise, nosed in at an angle in front of the cab.

It was a late model Pontiac, and the driver leaped out as it came to a full stop, circled the back of his car and came up to the cab and jerked open the back door.

"Is that you, Sutter?"

In the dim light of a street lamp half a block away, Sutter saw a thin black mustache across the young man's face peering in at him, and recognized Victor Conroy, the late Wesley Ames' private secretary.

He replied with some asperity, "Of course it is I. Who else do you expect to be cruising around this section of Miami at midnight in this fashion? Have you the documents we discussed over the telephone?"

"Right here." Conroy withdrew a thick envelope from his pocket. "What have you got for me in exchange?"

"Exactly what I promised you I would have," Sutter told him. He reached across the length of the back seat for the envelope Conroy held. "I'll have to check the contents before we conclude our deal."

Conroy drew back his hand and said grimly, "You can check mine while I check yours. Let's see the color of your money first."

At that moment the front door of the cab came open and the driver came out from behind the steering wheel all in one lithe movement. The man's figure was no longer slouched, but was tall and broad-shouldered, and Sutter saw the glint of blued-steel in his right hand and heard a harsh voice come from his lips that held no trace of a Southern drawl:

"All right, Conroy. Step back from the car with your hands in the air."

Before he had finished speaking the young man leaped at him. Perhaps he didn't see the gun in Michael Shayne's right hand, or perhaps he didn't care. His rush carried both of them back into the vee formed by the front fenders of the taxi and the Pontiac, and the vizored cap went spinning from Shayne's head, and Sutter saw his face and the red hair and realized for the first time who his driver had been.

He saw the rangy redhead straighten with his back against the front fender of the taxi, saw Conroy raining furious blows on his face and body, and saw Shayne swing the heavy automatic in his right hand against the side of the younger man's head where it made a smacking sound in the night and caused him to stagger back from the attack, and then Shayne calmly measured him with a straight left to the jaw which sent him backward and down like an expertly axed ox.

Shayne leaned down over him and impassively picked up the bulky envelope which had fallen from his fingers, and stepped to the open door of the taxi and leaned in to proffer it to the shaking attorney.

"Let's get this part of our business finished before Conroy comes around or anyone else turns up to start asking questions. Hand over the two envelopes you've got."

"But . . . but. . . ." stammered Sutter.

"No goddamned buts. I'll take the money. See if your stuff is all in here."

Dazed and bewildered and frightened, Sutter hesitantly withdrew the two envelopes containing currency from his pocket and silently passed them over to the detective and seized the envelope Shayne had taken from Conroy in return.

Shayne stepped back a pace and hastily thumbed through the contents of both envelopes, then wadded the money into his pocket and turned to kneel beside Conroy who was beginning to stir and groan on the pavement.

14

HE LIFTED THE LAX FIGURE OF THE SECRETARY AS easily as he would have lifted a rag doll, and draped him forward, face down, across the front fender and hood of the Pontiac while he shook him down carefully for a weapon.

He found no weapon, but in his right-hand jacket pocket Shayne encountered a key with a heavy metal tab attached to it which he took out and held up to the light. The key had the number 25 stamped on it, and the metal tag was inscribed: Motel Biscay Rest, with an address on Biscayne Boulevard north of 79th Street.

Shayne turned it over and over questioningly in his hands, then scowled down at Conroy's unconscious body. He dropped the motel key in his own pocket and checked the man's pulse, found it was strong but irregular, and that his breathing was steady.

He turned his head as the New York attorney emerged from the back seat of the taxi, and exclaimed, "You certainly did give me a surprise, Shayne. I had no idea you were impersonating the driver. Is the young man hurt badly?"

"Just knocked out. He'll come around soon enough. You get your stuff all right?"

"Yes. All the papers seem to be in order. What are you going to do with Conroy? Will he have to be charged with attempted blackmail, with me subpoenaed as a witness? After all no harm has really been done. I have the papers I came for. If this entire affair can possibly be kept quiet you will be doing my firm and our client a great service, and I assure you that adequate payment will be made."

"I've got a fairly adequate payment in my pocket already," Shayne told him bluntly. "I'll consider that my fee if I can keep this quiet. Unfortunately, though, it may be evidence against Conroy for murder, and you may be required to testify."

"Murder? I don't understand. I thought that was all settled."

"I told you things had changed. Here's what I advise you to do," Shayne went on swiftly. "Can you drive Conroy's car?"

"I presume so. It seems a standard model."

"Then get back to your hotel right away. No. You'd better stop some place. At another hotel lobby on the way where you can address that envelope and get some stamps for it. Put it in the mail for New York before you go to the Costain. Then leave the Pontiac parked a block or so away and go in and straight up to your room. The cops will either be waiting for you, or they'll be around soon. They'll be asking you questions about the period you were in the Ames house before he was shot, but we'll hope they have no lead on this and won't question you. Don't volunteer anything. Be evasive about where you've been since checking in at the Costain. If I can clear up Ames' murder in the meantime, there's no reason this blackmail caper has to enter into it. Just sit tight and hope you'll be allowed to take a morning plane to New York. Get in that car and drive it away so I can get out of here," he went on gruffly, turning back to Conroy and getting the limp body onto his shoulder.

He carried the man around to the other side of

the taxi and thrust him into the front seat where he huddled down in a crumpled heap, breathing stertorously but with his eyes still tightly closed.

Sutter was behind the steering wheel of the Pontiac starting the motor when Shayne hurried around and got into the cab. He got the other car moving, and headed sedately southward toward downtown Miami, and Shayne made a left turn in the taxi at the next corner and drove to Biscayne Boulevard where he turned north.

Victor Conroy began to stir and make funny noises, and try to lift his head on the seat beside him. Shayne watched him out of the corner of his eye while he drove at moderate speed in the right-hand lane of the almost deserted Boulevard. They were past 79th when Conroy managed to pull himself up and turn his head and blink dazedly at his companion.

"Wha . . . where are we? What happened?" he managed to blurt out. "You're . . . Mike Shayne, by God. You were driving that cab. I remember now."

"Keep right on remembering," Shayne said grimly. "You've got a lot of talking to do, Conroy." Ahead of them on the right, a high, arched neon sign spelled out BISCAY REST, and beneath that in smaller letters, Sorry—No Vacancy.

"My head," moaned Conroy, hunching forward and trying to retch, putting both hands up to his forehead. "What did you hit me with?"

"First a gun and then my fist," Shayne told him stolidly. He slowed to turn in to the motel entrance, drove past the darkened office to a U-shaped courtyard lined on three sides with connecting motel units. Parked cars stood in front of most of the doors, and at least ninety percent of the units were dark. Shayne checked the numbers on the doors and found 25 with an empty parking space in front of it and a night light on over the door.

Conroy lifted his head from his hands to look around apprehensively when the taxi stopped and Shayne cut off the motor. "Where are we?" he demanded, his voice thin with rising hysteria.

"End of the line," Shayne told him. "I think I'm about to pin a murder rap on you . . . maybe two." He leaned past him to unlatch the door, shoved him out roughly with a firm grip on his left arm.

"I didn't . . . kill anybody," stammered Conroy with his teeth chattering. "You've got it all wrong. He was dead when I went in there. I swear he was."

Shayne said, "Shut up. First we're going to take a look in number twenty-five. Then you can start talking."

He put the motel key in the lock and turned it, opened the door and dragged Conroy inside and pressed a wall switch by the door.

Overhead light showed a double bed and the figure of a woman lying on her back with arms outstretched. She was fully dressed and her eyes were closed and her face was very white.

It was Dorothy Larson.

Shayne shoved Conroy across the room away from him with such force that he struck the wall and slid to the floor. He jerked the door shut and bolted it and then took two strides to the side of the bed where he picked up one of Dorothy's wrists. It was limp, but it was warm, and there was a strong, steady pulse. She appeared to be in a deep, drugged sleep, but her lips came apart and she moaned faintly as Shayne bent over her, and her eyelids fluttered and then rested shut again.

Shayne straightened up and turned on Conroy who was picking himself up from the floor. "What did you use to knock her out?"

"A couple of sleeping pills," Conroy mumbled eagerly. "Just enough to keep her quiet until I could get back. They'll wear off pretty soon and she'll tell you. I didn't hurt her. She was just hysterical and I was afraid she might do something crazy. So I brought her here where she'd be safe from her husband. Don't you understand? That was before he came back and shot Wesley and got arrested. I thought he might come after her next. And I didn't know what she'd do or what she'd tell him. I was afraid to take a chance. Don't you understand what I'm saying?"

Shayne said, "Frankly, no." He moved back to a chair near the door and sat in it and got out a cigarette. "Was this after you stabbed Ames and stole the papers Sutter wanted?"

"I didn't stab him." Conroy sank into a chair across the room and looked at him wide-eyed, the picture of innocence. "You did find that out finally, huh? I wondered when you and that sergeant came back. He wouldn't tell any of us why he was reopening the case when we all thought he had it wrapped up with Ralph Larson as the Killer. And then you asked about the paper-knife."

"Is that what you used?" Shayne asked levelly.

"I tell you I didn't. I went in his study and he was dead. I could see he'd been stabbed in the heart, and I thought of course that Ralph Larson had done it. Why shouldn't I think that?" he demanded heatedly. "He was the last one who'd been up the back way to see him. We all knew that Ralph suspected Wesley was laying his wife. You could hear them arguing in there and then Ralph went out the back, and when I went in fifteen minutes later, Wesley was dead. Naturally, I thought Ralph had done it. You don't know how mixed up I felt later when I came back to the house and discovered Ralph had broken in with a pistol and shot Ames after I knew he was already dead. What could I *say?* All I could do was keep my mouth shut and hope that was the end of it. What did it matter whether Ralph was electrocuted for stabbing or shooting him . . . or both? Though I still don't understand why he came back to shoot a man he had already killed with a paperknife."

"Let's back-track a little bit," said Shayne reasonably. "You claim you heard them arguing and Ralph leave . . . and you went in the study a few minutes later and found Ames stabbed to death. Is that your story?"

"It's the truth. I knew that envelope was in his desk with the Murchinson file that Sutter had flown down here to get. I knew Sutter was prepared to pay twenty-five thousand in cash for those papers. So I grabbed the envelope quick and just walked out and pulled the door shut behind me. I knew Ralph had killed him, of course, and why. And I was afraid of what Ralph might do to Dorothy after killing Ames. Or what she might tell him if he came back to her and admitted he had killed Ames. Having killed once on her account, the damned fool might well come after me if she broke down and admitted to him that he'd killed the wrong man. I had to get to her before he did and shut her up, don't you see?"

Shayne said slowly, "I'm beginning to see . . . a little. Do you mean it was you she was having an affair with . . . not Ames?"

"Of course. Do you think she'd look at a popinjay like that? The funny thing was, Ames understood the situation and rather enjoyed it. He knew Ralph suspected him, and I think he actually egged

Ralph on to believe it. It pleased his goddamned ego to have Ralph think that a beautiful woman like Dorothy was in love with him."

"So you went straight to the Larson apartment after you left Ames dead in his study and walked out with the Murchinson file?"

"Yes. I wanted to get the papers out of the house before Wesley's death was discovered so I could make a deal with Sutter later, and I didn't know what Ralph might do after killing Ames. You can imagine how I felt until I got to Dorothy." Victor Conroy drew in a deep breath at the memory and released it slowly, shaking his head.

"I didn't know whether I'd find Ralph there, or what. But Dorothy was alone, and practically hysterical. She clung to me and babbled that Ralph was going to kill Ames and I should stop him, and I didn't realize what she was talking about and I told her he already had killed him. Then she went all to pieces and began to blame me for everything. I couldn't leave her alone in that state. I knew she needed time to get to her senses before she talked to anybody. And I needed time to collect from Sutter. With that amount of cash in my pocket I meant to simply disappear and take Dorothy with me. First she agreed to go with me and started to pack a bag, and then she suddenly changed her mind and got martyr-like and swore she was going to tell the whole world the truth and share Ralph's guilt with him. I couldn't let it be like that. Don't you see I couldn't? I knew she'd come to her senses later on if she had a chance to think about it calmly. So we wrestled a little and I . . . well, I hit her," Conroy confessed shamefacedly. "I didn't mean to but her nose bled dreadfully and she was crying and taking on and we mopped it up in the bathroom and then she sort of collapsed and came with me. I gave her a drink with two of her sleeping powders in it and she didn't notice, and she came here where I rented this room, and by the time I got her in here she was practically asleep on her feet. You can see that's all that's the matter with her." Conroy gestured toward the bed, sounding run down now, and exhausted. "She'll tell you the same thing when she wakes up. I didn't hurt her. I was in love with her. All I wanted was time enough to make a deal with Sutter and get travelling money. If I'd known at the time that Ralph was already under arrest for shooting Wesley, I wouldn't have worried about her and about getting her away from there. But I didn't know that until I left her here and went back to the house."

"What did you think when you got there and found out what had happened?"

"I didn't know what to think. I was so sure Ralph had stabbed him. No man in his right mind would come back and openly shoot a dead man. And then I thought maybe he wasn't in his right mind. That he'd gone nuts and didn't know what he was doing the second time."

"What makes you so sure Ralph stabbed him?"

"But he *must* have. Who else was there? He was the only one who'd been in the study."

"Did you pull the paper-knife out of Ames ... and bolt the back door?" Shayne asked evenly.

"I didn't touch anything. I didn't see any paper-knife. He was just leaning back in his chair grinning sort of. With blood on the front of him."

"Didn't you notice that the back door was bolted on the inside?" demanded Shayne.

"No. It couldn't have been. Ralph went out that way." Victor Conroy looked at him aghast.

"It was bolted on the inside half an hour later when Ralph ran in the front door of the study and shot him."

"I don't see how . . . you're making that up to trick me. I didn't kill Wesley Ames."

"Ralph Larson couldn't possibly have done it and left that door bolted behind him," Shayne told him coldly. "That leaves somebody inside the house after Ralph left. Five of you altogether, counting the houseman. You're the one who had most to gain. You knew Sutter had twenty-five grand he was prepared to hand over for the Murchinson file. You admit you were in the room and stole the file. We've got you dead to rights on that. What did you do with the knife, Conroy?"

"I didn't kill him," cried out Conroy, beating his fist on his knee in frustration and anger. "I didn't see any knife. I grabbed the papers on the spur of the moment. They weren't any good to any one else. Damn it! If Ralph Larson didn't kill him, take a look at some of the others in the house. Ask Mark Ames why he was there tonight. I happen to know it was to demand that Wesley give Helena a divorce. Ask *her*. God knows she had plenty of motive to kill the son-of-a-bitch. How about that New York lawyer? He was plenty sore and half drunk. He had plenty of chance to slip in and do it. And I wouldn't put it past Alfred either. God, the way Wesley treated that man like dirt. A knife is a Spick's weapon. Any of the others had a motive and opportunity." He was practically shouting as he completed his diatribe, and the drugged woman on the bed stirred and muttered something and turned on her side.

Shayne got up to go over to her, telling Conroy as he did so, "But *you're* the one we can place in the death room just about the time it happened." He leaned over the bed and placed a firm hand on Dorothy Larson's shoulder and shook her gently.

"Better try to wake up," he said soothingly. "It's all right. Everything's okay. Wake up and I'll take you home."

She turned slowly to open her eyes and stare up into his face, blankly and uncomprehendingly at first, and then with troubled recognition.

"You're... the detective," she mumbled. "Ralph? What's happened to Ralph?" Then she sat up suddenly and stared with distended eyes at Conroy who was approaching the bed hesitantly. "Victor said he killed Wesley," she cried out. "Did he? Did Ralph do that?"

Shayne said heavily, "Right now, Mrs. Larson, your husband is in jail charged with shooting Wesley Ames to death. But I think that charge is going to be withdrawn before long. Just lie back and relax. After I make a telephone call you can tell me exactly what happened in your apartment tonight."

He lifted the telephone from the bedside stand and gave the number for police headquarters, and put his hand over the mouthpiece and told Conroy coldly. "Stay away from her. Sit down and keep your mouth shut."

He lifted his hand and spoke into the telephone, "Mike Shayne speaking. I'm at number twenty-five in the Biscay Rest Motel on Biscayne Boulevard and I've got a suspect here in the Ames killing. Have a car stop by to pick him up. And if you can get hold of Sergeant Griggs, tell him he can stop looking for Mrs. Larson. I've got her, too."

He hung up and looked down compassionately at Dorothy Larson who had rolled over and buried her face in her hands and was weeping violently. For her husband... or for her lover, he wondered. It didn't seem to much matter. Nothing was going to be the same for her again.

15

THIS TIME THERE WAS EVIDENTLY A CAR CRUISING VERY near-by because it was not more than three minutes before one pulled into the courtyard silently with a flashing red light and eased up behind the taxi parked in front of No. 25.

Shayne opened the door as two burly, uniformed men got purposefully out of the radio car. "This way," he called cheerfully, and was pleased to recognize the one in the lead as an officer whom he knew slightly.

He held the door open and stood aside and said, "Hi, Thompson. That was quick work."

"They said Mike Shayne over the radio," Thompson said guardedly, peering inside the motel room. "What's going on here? Vice charge?"

"I've got a murder suspect for Sergeant Griggs on the Ames killing," Shayne told him. "That's Victor Conroy. Take him in, Tommy, and hold him on an open charge until I get there. I have to take Mrs. Larson home and I'll be right in. If Griggs is at headquarters tell him to stay put until I get there."

Conroy went with the two officers silently and sullenly. He had kept his eyes averted from Dorothy Larson and had not exchanged a word with her since she had waked up. She, in turn, appeared too stunned and shocked to comprehend exactly what was going on, and after the patrol car drove away with her lover, Shayne took her arm to draw her up from the bed and said gently, "I've got a taxi outside, Mrs. Larson. I'll take you home now."

"Yes," she agreed falteringly, clinging to him. "It's like a bad dream. Ralph running in to get his gun, and then I telephoned you, didn't I? And then Victor came and said . . . that Ralph had murdered Wesley Ames. . . ." Her voice trailed off uncertainly and Shayne helped her into the back seat and got under the wheel and drove out of the courtyard.

"Just sit back and relax now," he said over his shoulder. "Ralph did fire a bullet into Ames, but it now develops that he was dead before the shot was fired."

"Then . . . he didn't actually murder him?" she asked wonderingly. "I'm glad. It would be my fault if he had."

Shayne said, "Don't think about it now. When we get to your place I want you to tell me briefly just what you remember. If you confirm Conroy's story . . . well, we'll see."

When they climbed the stairway to her apartment Shayne fully expected to see a policeman guarding her door. But the hallway was empty and the door opened when he turned the knob. He was surprised to find Griggs standing in the center of the room talking to his driver, and from the expression on the sergeant's face when he saw Shayne and Dorothy, he realized that Griggs knew nothing about her being found or Conroy's arrest.

He held her arm and said, "This is Dorothy Larson, Sergeant Griggs. The sergeant is in charge of the case," he explained to her, and went on to Griggs, "She's been through a lot tonight. I think she's eager to make a brief statement that will clarify a lot of things. Why don't you get that first and then we can leave her alone and I'll fill you in with the rest of it."

Griggs nodded and gestured toward a comfortable

chair. "Sit down, Mrs. Larson. You had us pretty badly worried about you . . . with blood all over and you mysteriously missing."

She sank into the chair and smiled wanly, her face very white and strained, but in control of herself. "I didn't know . . . what to do. I was so upset and frightened when Ralph ran out with his gun saying he was going to kill Mr. Ames. And then Victor came and told me Ralph *had* killed him. . . ." She paused, twisting her hands together in her lap and blinking back tears.

Griggs looked at Shayne with raised eyebrows and a scowl of utter bafflement. "Victor? How the devil did he know . . . ?"

"Conroy is being held at headquarters waiting for us to question him," Shayne explained. "The way he tells it: He discovered Ames' dead body in the study and thought Ralph had done it on his first trip, and he panicked and rushed over here to Mrs. Larson because he was actually her lover instead of Ames and he was afraid she would get hysterical and blurt out the truth to Ralph if he wasn't here to prevent it."

"Is that true, Mrs. Larson? Were you and Victor Conroy lovers?"

"It's true enough. It just happened . . . and Ralph got the idea somehow that it was Wesley Ames I was seeing. That's why it was so utterly horrible when he ran out with his gun to kill Wesley. It was the wrong man, don't you see? I tried to stop him . . . I tried to tell him . . . but he didn't hear a word I said."

Sergeant Griggs drew in a deep breath, pondering and evaluating this information. "What did Conroy say and do when he came here?"

"He was excited and he asked where Ralph was

and I told him he'd gone out threatening to kill Wesley, and he said he'd already done it and it wasn't safe for me to stay here, and for me to pack a bag and come with him to hide some place where Ralph couldn't find me until he was safely under arrest.

"I hardly knew what I was doing. I started to pack a bag and go with him, and then I suddenly thought how it was all my fault and I couldn't run away and desert Ralph like that. But Victor got furious and insisted and tried to force me to go on packing my bag, and we wrestled in the bedroom and that's when I got a nose-bleed. And then I just hardly know," she ended helplessly. "I gave in and said all right, and he washed my face and gave me a drink, and helped me down the stairs to his car and we drove off.

"Things got fuzzy while we were driving and I dimly remember going into a room and lying down on a bed. And then I didn't know anything until Mr. Shayne was standing over me and shaking me awake."

"He doped her with some of her own sleeping powders," Shayne told Griggs. "He said he gave her two of them, but it must have been more to have acted so fast. I don't believe he meant her any harm. He just wanted her out of the way and incommunicado until he could get back to the house and brazen it out when Ames' body was found."

"Not knowing at that point that Ralph had come back with a gun to shoot a dead man?"

"He couldn't have known anything about that, according to the timing. Naturally, he kept his mouth tightly shut when he did walk in and learn that Ralph had been arrested for murder."

"Naturally," agreed Griggs grimly. "He must have

felt pretty damn good and smug about things at that point."

He turned to Mrs. Larson and said in a curiously gentle voice: "I think that's all we need from you for now. Will you be all right alone here? I could leave a man, if you like."

"Why shouldn't I be all right? You . . . you think Victor did it, don't you?"

"I don't rightly know what we think at this point," Griggs told her. "You got some more sleeping pills if you need them?"

Dorothy Larson shuddered. "I'm sure there are some, though I don't think I'll ever take another one. Why don't you go on? I'd like to be alone."

As the three men went down the stairs together, Shayne asked the sergeant, "Did you latch onto anything new after I left the Ames house?"

"Nothing worth a damn. Going over their stories a second time just left things in the same mess. They all denied hearing anything from the study during the crucial half hour. I didn't tell them about the stab wound, of course. Theoretically the only person who knows about that is the one who stabbed him. Now you tell me Conroy knew all the time he'd been stabbed. Why didn't he tell us in the beginning if he was innocent?"

"I guess he thought it was better just to let well enough alone when he found Larson charged with the crime anyhow. His story is that he was convinced that Larson was the knife-slayer."

"How could he be when that back door was bolted on the inside?"

"Conroy didn't know about that . . . he says." Shayne paused, "What are you doing about Sutter?"

"Nothing yet," fumed Griggs. "*He* seems to be missing too. Checked in at a hotel all right, but he still hadn't turned up in his room the last I heard from the man I sent to bring him in."

Shayne said casually, "I doubt that he'll have anything useful to contribute." They had stopped at the curb beside the sergeant's car, and the taxi Shayne had been using was parked three cars behind it. Not wishing to draw Griggs' attention to his unorthodox conveyance, Shayne opened the door for the sergeant and suggested, "You go ahead on in. I'll follow right along because I want to sit in when you question Conroy."

Griggs said reluctantly, "I guess you earned that." He stooped to enter his car and paused in that position, "You haven't told me how you got onto him . . . and his having Mrs. Larson stashed away in a motel room."

"I'll tell you all about it later," Shayne told him breezily, striding away. "Pure coincidence. Just one of my lucky hunches."

He walked past the taxi slowly, turned and came back to it as the Homicide car pulled away. He followed at a moderate pace and parked the cab unobtrusively around the corner from the police station in front of an all night short order joint, and walked back to climb the one flight of stairs to Griggs' office.

He found the sergeant seated alone at his desk, and he almost beamed as he told the redhead, "I think maybe we got some kind of break, though I'm damned if I see how it adds up right now. But it's sure as hell a tie-in between Sutter and Victor Conroy. You know I had a man waiting at Sutter's hotel for him to show up. I sent Powers because he knew him by sight. I just had a call from Powers when I walked in a minute ago. He was waiting outside the hotel when a Pontiac pulled up and Sutter got out of it. He refused to tell Powers where he'd been the last hour, and you know what?"

With a sinking heart Shayne realized that he did, indeed, "know what." But he concealed his knowledge and asked weakly, "What, Sergeant?"

"It was Victor Conroy's car that Sutter was driving. I knew there was something fishy about that lawyer all along. I'll get the truth out of him now. What he was really doing in Miami and what his business was with Ames."

"Yeh," said Shayne, suddenly very conscious of the fact that he had twenty-five thousand dollars of blackmail money wadded into his right-hand pants pocket.

"While we're waiting for him," he said desperately, "how about having Conroy and Larson in?"

"They're both on their way right now. One thing I want to ask Conroy before Sutter gets here is what the lawyer was doing driving his car."

"As a matter of fact, I can explain that," Shayne said quickly. "Remember asking me how I found Conroy and Mrs. Larson in the motel room? It was this way...."

He paused, cudgeling his brain for a plausible explanation that would satisfy the sergeant and sidetrack him from his present line of inquiry which was bound to expose the blackmail angle and his questionable part in it.

Before he was able to think of anything the door opened and a policeman ushered Ralph Larson into the room. He was still sullen-faced and defiant, and he looked at Griggs curiously as the sergeant leaned back in his chair and smiled benignly.

"You're a lucky son-of-a-gun, Larson!"

"I am?" He looked bewildered. "Why?"

"Because we've got a damned efficient police department in Miami, and we leave no stones unturned in seeking the solution of a crime." Griggs spoke sonorously and Shayne realized he must have memorized his little speech carefully. "First though," Griggs went on, thoroughly enjoying himself, "if you're still worried about your wife . . . forget it. She's safely back at home. I left her there myself not more than fifteen minutes ago."

"That's fine," muttered Ralph. "I'm . . . glad."

"Secondly," said Griggs, "you didn't shoot Wesley Ames to death tonight even though you did try like hell. Do you know *why* you didn't, Larson?"

"He knows why all right," Shayne said coldly. "Stop toying with him, Sergeant. He's the one man in Miami who knew that Wesley Ames was dead before he fired that bullet into his heart because he had stabbed him to death half an hour earlier.

"You were damned smart to figure that out so fast, Sergeant," Shayne hurried on with a chuckle while Griggs regarded him in openmouthed astonishment and Larson scowled blackly and tried to break in with a protest.

"Remember right there in the study when we discovered the paper-knife was missing, you theorized that Ralph had stabbed him on his first trip and then hurried home to get a gun and come back and establish a perfect alibi by pretending to shoot him. It was damned fast and clever thinking, Larson," Shayne told him, "after you realized you were the only and the perfect suspect for the stabbing. But you almost made a fatal mistake by placing your bullet in the same hole the knife had gone into. That's what the sergeant meant by the efficiency of the police department. If you'd killed him by *shooting* it would have shown premeditation and been first degree murder. And that would really have been ironic. Because, as it stands now, a jury will take into consideration the fact that you grabbed up that paper-knife in a jealous rage that brought on temporary insanity, and you'll probably get only a few years in prison. That's why you're a lucky son-of-a-gun. Because Sergeant Griggs refused to take even all the obvious facts for granted and ordered the post mortem that proved Ames was stabbed to death before he was shot."

Shayne paused to catch his breath, and saw Griggs shaking his bald head at him, sadly and reproachfully.

"You're forgetting something, Mike. I figured it might be like you say until you reminded me that the back door was bolted on the inside and that proved Ames had to be alive when Larson left."

"That's right," the young man put in shakily. "My God, I don't understand what you're talking about. If Ames *was* stabbed before I shot him, I certainly don't know anything about it. He was alive when I left, and I heard him bolt that door behind me."

"Tell him, Sergeant," said Shayne indulgently.

"Tell him what, Mike?" Griggs looked more baffled than ever.

"That we found *his* fingerprints on that inside back door bolt . . . and then we knew exactly how he worked it. You ran to that back door and bolted it *before* you fired at the dead man," Shayne told Larson with a shrug.

"It was obvious when we found traces of your fingerprints on it. That's why you bothered to lock the front door behind you when you ran in. To give yourself a few precious seconds to bolt the back door before you shot him."

"I didn't! This is all absolutely haywire. I swear I don't understand. . . ."

"As soon as Conroy comes in," Shayne said to

Griggs, "ask him how Larson was dressed when he came to see Ames. One will get you ten he was wearing a jacket. He was expecting to go out on an assignment for Ames tonight among the night spots, and even in Miami they require jackets in most places. But he was in his shirt-sleeves when he came *back* to shoot Ames. Why? Why would he get rid of his jacket in the meantime? I'll tell you why. Because when he stabbed Ames he unconsciously dropped the paper-knife in his coat pocket and ran out with it. Send a man out to his apartment and have his wife look in the closet for the jacket he wore to work this morning. Ten to one, it'll be hanging there. It would seem safer to him than trying to throw it away and he was racing against time to get back and shoot Ames before he was discovered dead. And one will get you ten that there'll be traces of Ames' blood in the coat pocket. Not the knife, maybe. That would be easy to toss out the car window."

Ralph Larson was backing away in horror as Shayne spoke, and he cowered against the wall with both hands over his face. Griggs looked at him with a scowl and said softly, "By God, Mike, I swear you hit the nail on the head that time. I wouldn't give you one against a hundred that there isn't blood inside that jacket pocket."

There was a sharp rap on the door and Patrolman Powers opened it and stood on the threshold holding firmly to Sutter's arm. "Here he is, Sarge."

"Take him away," said Griggs absently. "We're busy in here, Son. Let him go. What the hell do I care whose car he was driving tonight? We just solved a murder, Mike Shayne and I. I don't care what he was doing in Miami just so he wasn't killing anybody."

16

BEHIND THE WHEEL OF HIS BORROWED TAXICAB AGAIN, Shayne drove east to Miami Avenue and turned south a block to park directly behind his own car which was at the curb in front of a dingy bar-room. He took the keys out of the ignition and dropped them into his pocket, then withdrew the wad of crumpled bills given to him so unwillingly by Alonzo Sutter, and selected one for five hundred dollars from the others.

He put that in the pocket with the taxi keys and shoved the rest of the money back into his other pocket, and then got out briskly and entered the bar-room. There were half a dozen late drinkers seated on stools, and Shayne circled them to seat himself at the end beside a stocky man with a pock-marked face and a cheerful grin.

The man glanced at him casually as he sat down, and when the bartender moved down in front of them he said heartily, "Bring my friend a slug of cognac if you've got such in the house, Jim. With ice water on the side. Everything okay, Mike?" he added as the bartender turned away.

"All through," Shayne told him. "Your heap is parked outside behind mine. Trade keys, huh?" He got the taxi keys from his pocket and put them on the bar, and the stocky man got Shayne's car keys out and exchanged them for his own.

The bartender set a shot-glass of cognac in front

of the redhead with a glass of ice water beside it. Shayne took a sip and continued in a conversational tone: "Only one casualty. I lost your cap somewhere along the line. And I ran up a few bucks on your meter that you'll have to turn in." He withdrew the wadded five-hundred bill from his pocket and slid it in front of the taxi-driver.

The man spread it out slowly on the mahogany, protesting, "That was an old cap, Mike. You don't hafta...." He paused, looking down at the denomination of the bill. "Holy gee! Is that two goddamn zeroes I'm looking at?"

Shayne said happily, "That's right. Hacking was real profitable tonight. Buy your old lady a fur coat or something." He tossed off the rest of his drink and chased it with water, stood up and put his left hand firmly on the stocky man's shoulder. "Thanks for the drink."

He went out and got into his own car, started the motor and glanced at his watch. He had promised Lucy Hamilton he would let her know how things turned out if it wasn't too late. He decided it wasn't too late, and he turned east in the direction of her apartment.

The lights were all out in the front windows of her second-floor apartment when he parked in front of the building, and he got out his key-ring as he entered the small foyer, and selected from it a key which Lucy had given him for emergencies many years ago, but which he had not used more than two or three times in all those years.

It unlocked the outer door for him, and he went in and climbed one flight of stairs, and the same key unlocked the door of her apartment.

He went into the entry-hall and switched on the ceiling light in the living room, entered through the archway and hesitated momentarily when he saw it was empty and her bedroom door was closed.

Then he thrust his hand deep into his pocket and fingered the wad of bills there, strode blithely across to the door and opened it.

Enough light entered Lucy's bedroom from behind him to show the outline of her body curled up beneath the covers on the bed, and Shayne walked quietly to her side and looked down at her face pressed against the pillow.

She was sleeping peacefully and trustfully, just as she had been earlier that night when he returned to his apartment, and again he stood beside her for a long moment, looking down at her and remembering a lot of things.

Then he brought his hand out of his pocket and held it high in the air over her head and began letting thousands of dollars begin fluttering down over her.

She stirred as some of the bills settled gently on her face, and opened her eyes slowly to look up into his grinning face, and then she sat up quickly, brushing the bills away and looking at them in bewilderment on the bedspread in front of her.

She looked up at him again, shaking her tousled head gravely, and told him with a catch in her voice, "A mink coat doesn't cost that much money, Michael."

His grin widened and he opened his big fist to let the rest of the money fall into her lap. He said generously, "Then let's make it ermine, angel. Get yourself into a robe while I fix us both a drink and tell you what a smart guy you're working for."